Advance Praise

"Life as a young adolescent is fraught with a daily gauntlet of socioemotional events while searching for genuine identities that fit! In L. E. A. P., Bellon captures the emotions that run on a loop through 14-year-old Linn's mind as she navigates friends, her brother, dad, and her mercurial mom who's fighting her own demons in a never-ending war. Bellon's dry humor with lines such as, "The Fourth of July always has sales, and I need some new genes" will keep you LYAO; but Linn's reality digs deeply into your soul as you cheer for her to find solace in a seemingly impossible journey toward adulthood. You'll laugh and cry as Bellon's story telling places you directly into the uncertainty of adolescence—that feeling of being frozen in time between the joys of ignorant childhood and the promise of ever-elusive adult-like opportunities—"juvenescence" as Bellon labels it."

Dave F. Brown, EdD., young adolescent researcher and author of Young Adolescents and the Middle Schools They Need.

"Funny and tragic, poignant and powerful, Bellon draws on personal experience to weave the tale of a mother-daughter relationship strained to the point of breaking by mom's alcoholism. But search beneath those tumultuous waves to find perhaps the real story: an inspiring and realistic depiction of sibling survival against the odds."

Chris Negron, acclaimed author of Underdog City, The Last Super Chef, and Dan Unmasked

"Thirteen-year-old Linn is a liar, and, in her family, this is an asset. Everyone lies to keep the 'perfect family' illusion intact. But only two people think the illusion is working and they are Linn's parents. Changing would require acknowledging that Linn's mother is an alcoholic and neither of her parents is ready for that. Linn and her brother Brendan do what is required to survive in an unpredictable and unsupportive home. Above all else, they must pretend to be perfect, even as their problems worsen.

L.E.A.P.: Linn's Emerging Adult Plan by Toni Bellon is an honest view into the life of a teen living with an alcoholic parent and the systemic dysfunction that happens in a family that tries to pretend everything is normal. Readers will love Linn and her insightful, pragmatic nature. Bellon is a masterful storyteller and Linn's journey toward adulthood is entertaining, heartbreaking, and hopeful."

Kim Ottesen, Programming Manager, Forsyth County Public Library

L.E.A.P.

LINN'S
~~GROWING~~
EMERGING
ADULT
~~LIST~~
PLAN

by
Toni Bellon

KINKAJOU PRESS

ISBN: 9781951122911 (paperback) / 9781951122928 (ebook)
LCCN: 2024933359

Kinkajou Press
9 Mockingbird Hill Rd
Tijeras, New Mexico 87059
info@kinkajoupress.com
www.kinkajoupress.com

Content Warning: This book contains descriptions of alcoholism, verbal and psychological abuse, and physical abuse that may be disturbing to some readers. It includes discussions of suicide and menstration (periods).

For my children and grandchildren, birthed or chosen.
You are safe and loved.

Dedicated to Sonja Kozuch,
the definition of a great friend.

Acknowledgements

This book would not exist if it weren't for my brother, Joe, and all the guilt I've felt about his life situation. Sorry, Bro. I did the best I could.

I have benefited from the advice of editors and professional readers such as Lisa McCoy (Lisa McCoy Editing), Hannah Van Vels Ausbury, Deborah Halverson, and Kyra Nelson. As well as Beta Readers Veronica Coons, Ranae Lubertazzi, Amanda Wilkerson, Michelle Tompkins, and Justin Vilonna. Eternal thanks to my publisher and best editor, Geoff Habiger. Your calming tone helped me stay sane.

Within this story, I found areas I needed more information about. Then I reached out to Michael Wilkerson for help with teen communication. My educational consultants were Lorie and Dusty Skorich. You all gave great advice; any mistakes are totally mine.

To any writer, I'd say "Find a critique group or two." People from the Forsyth County Writer's Group were invaluable. Thanks to Heather Elrod, Nicole Collier Harp, Chris Negron, Kim Ottesen, Leo Penha, Meg Robinson, Rich Smith, Michelle Tompkins, and Justin Vilonna. From the Roswell Critique Group, I'd like to thank Pat Bowen, Olga Jackson, Jeremy Logan, Meg Ratcliff, Brenda Sevcik, John Sheffield, Jan Slimming, and Susan Swann. The Atlanta Writers Club and Conference have been more than helpful. Thanks to George Weinstein and all the members/speakers involved.

Most importantly, I'd like to thank my husband, John Jupin, who has read about and lived with every word and character in Linn's world. Just maybe he's represented poorly in things I've written. Sorry, not sorry!

Toni Bellon

JOURNAL ENTRY –
SURVIVING MOTHER'S DAY

I got through Mother's Day this year without having anything thrown at me—objects or words. What do you say when everyone thinks your mother's a caring kindergarten teacher? You don't—you keep your mouth shut and pretend she's perfect. I'll be fourteen in four months. Brendan's older, but not by much. He thinks our family values are about keeping secrets. So, I lie and hide the truth from my friends and myself. My truth? I'd change the old poem—when she's good, she's okay, but when she drinks, she's a monster.

Linn

Walker

Gurke

Chapter 1
Teening Up

SITTING ON MY BED, I review my new journal entry. Is this what Grandma Rose wanted when she sent the notebook for my birthday last year? Her letter said I should find "positive truths in my life." Grandma wrote about starting every day thinking positive thoughts. Like, being lucky to be alive and having enough space to live in. Her letter explained that she'd been wanting a cow and the positives worked when a farmer friend gave her one. She named the cow 'Jed' so she wouldn't miss Grandpa after he'd passed. I'm not sure that was a truth. I mean, she got the cow, true. It's also true that my grandfather died three years ago. But, I'm pretty sure Grandpa Jed didn't want a cow named after him.

I'm just not sure wanting a cow is a positive. I heard that 'Jed the cow' didn't stay long. After Grandpa Jed died, Grandma moved to a smaller house. She kept 'Jed the cow' in her backyard and her neighborhood didn't allow people to have fences. The HOA didn't say anything about keeping cows. I doubt they imagined a person might want livestock. Jed became a problem with other residents and Grandma had to give the cow back to the farmer. Still, I try to follow her lead.

At first, I used the notebook she sent as a diary.

Dear Diary,

Today I started rereading <u>Johnny Tremain</u>. I read it five times in fourth grade and wanted to see if I still think it's good. It starts by describing animals. But what fourth grader reads a book that has the word 'cock' on the first page—twice? I must have been completely bonkers.

Dear Diary,

Why do I listen to boy singers? Because I listen to my older brother's music? I need to add girls to my playlist. But I don't like gooey love songs. Mom and Dad like 90s stuff—and opera. WTF? I need to find my style. Check out—angry girls and anthem songs.

Dear Diary,

Golden Boy talked to me today. Okay, he only said hello, but he looked at me. Nadine was there so I couldn't pee my pants without her noticing. Totally acted like it was no big deal.

In a few months, I'll be fourteen and in high school. High school means growing up and leaving childish things behind, like my diary entries. I've got to be more serious. Calling it a journal instead of a diary is more mature. Everything I wrote in my diary was true, but I don't think it's what Grandma meant. She wants me to write about *the truths in my life.*

Okay, I left the word *positive* out. Sorry, Grandma Rose, I know you want me to focus on what's good in my life, but you also want honesty. I'm not allowed to be honest about Mom. If I could tell Grandma the truth about Mom's drinking, she might understand why I lie. I mean, she should know her child's pulling the Bruce Banner to Hulk switch. I put my *journal* away when I hear the doorbell. That'll be Nadine. Even though she's my best friend—only friend—I don't want anyone to read about my truth. I've never told Nadine about Mom's big secret. And she hasn't seen what happens when Mom drinks. Let her believe Mom's a sweet kindergarten teacher. Isn't it better to protect Nadine from a mean drunk who isn't her problem?

"Thanks for coming," I say as soon as the door is open.

Nadine glances around. "Where's your parents? Don't they get today off too?"

"No. It's a teacher training day." I imagine Mom grabbing her tumbler and pouring a drink when she gets home. "Boring, with a capital B."

"So, it's only us?" Nadine asks.

"Nope. Brendan's here."

"Did I hear my name?" Brendan says as he enters the family room. "You girls talking about me? I know it's difficult to be in the same house with this awesomeness and control yourself." Brendan runs his hands up and down his sides.

I roll my eyes. "We're going to my room, and you're not invited." I turn and walk toward the garage. Nadine gives Brendan a finger wave.

My bedroom's the smallest one in the house. All the others are on the opposite side of the family room. My room is next to the laundry area and guest bathroom. Except when my parents pass my door on their way to or from the garage, I'm away from everyone else. I love the privacy.

Nadine sits on my bed, and I pull out my desk chair. Not a lot of choices here. My room has a twin bed, a desk, and a lilac beanbag chair. If it weren't for the beanbag, this room would disappear in a haze of bland. The last time we painted, Dad must've found a sale on beige.

"I need some help," I admit.

"Help?" Nadine laughs. "Linn's asking for help? Do you feel sick?" She becomes more serious when I laugh at her joke. "What do you need?"

My face turns red. "I need help buying bras."

"Glad to hear you're ready. I thought it was such a big deal when I started wearing a bra two years ago in sixth grade." Nadine grins. "Mom called them training bras."

"What does she think you're training them to do? Swim? Is that how you win all those races?" I give Nadine an exaggerated up and down look. "Are you still wearing your mom's *training* bra?"

"Funny, Linn, very funny." Nadine laughs. "This year I bought some racer-back mesh bras. They keep things in place and the colors match my underwear, in case."

"In case of what?" I ask.

"High school boys. I'm planning to 'show and tell' my pretty bra and matching undies. I'll walk up to the first guy I meet and ask if he likes lacey things." Nadine sticks her barely noticeable boobs out and laughs.

"Like that'll happen!" I snort and we both giggle. "Would your mom say I need a *training* bra? Could I teach mine to do math?"

"Linn, you need a full-on bra. Hasn't your mom suggested going shopping?"

"I asked her. She freaked out, announced the topic didn't exist, and left the room." I shake my head. "Mom's father was a religious nut. He blamed women for everything that's wrong with the world. You know, the whole Adam-and-Eve-apple-means-sex thing? So, the minute I started... growing... changing, Mom had problems with me."

"I'm sorry to hear that," Nadine says quietly. "What can I do to help?"

I'm too aware of my full-length mirror staring at me. "Help me buy bras? I don't know what I'm doing."

"We can go to Mercado Plaza. I've done this with my mother, lots. I can run sizes and types for you." Nadine beams. "I'll be your personal shopper."

"I'm not sure." I peek at the mirror. "I don't think I should be seen in public. I know I've been growing, but I've become someone I don't know and I don't like anything I see. Especially the zit taking over my chin." *Note to self—get rid of mirror.* "I can see my old self hiding in this bigger body. This year I've added two shoe sizes and five inches. All still ugly."

"No, Linn." Nadine stands and walks in front of me. "Your hair has cool blond and brown streaks. Those freckles are cute, and your eyes change color depending on what you wear. Did you see the way Steve was checking you out in gym class? I did."

"Steve looks at every girl," I point out.

Nadine wrinkles her forehead. "Steve doesn't pay attention to me and I'm a girl."

"Then he's stupid. You're way prettier than I am."

"Who's prettier than who?" Brendan asks as he walks into my room.

"Brendan," I sigh. "Get out!"

"Chill, Lil Sislet. I only popped in to check my hair." Brendan leans in front of me to see his reflection in the mirror. He strokes a strand of perfectly placed hair. Brendan loves everything he sees. How am I related to this guy?

"You two aren't doing anything private." Brendan squints at Nadine. "Right, Nad-D?"

"That's right, Bunny Buns." Nadine gives Brendan a fake smile. "Nothing to see here. Simply two girls planning a juvenescence shopping trip. You can hop along now."

"Juvie-scents?" Brendan questions. "What's that?"

"It means growing up." Nadine arches one eyebrow at Brendan. "You know, the time when you're changing from a child into an adult. My parents use big words all the time to increase my vocabulary. Don't yours?"

"Nope." Brendan ignores Nadine's sarcasm and lowers himself into my beanbag chair. "We speak English here. While you're doing your juvie shopping, get Spaz here some battle armor." Brendan nods his head toward me.

"Juvie? Battle armor?" I ask.

"You know." Brendan shrugs. "You need a shortstop to protect second base."

Nadine rolls her eyes. "Brendan, you're totally cringe-worthy." She turns to me. "He's saying you need a bra."

"What? How do you... Who said... Have you been... I can't even." I cover my face.

"Chillax Bubbles." Brendan looks back and forth between Nadine and me. "You two will be in high school soon. I can't have my idiot little sister shaking *the goods* across campus. I have a reputation to maintain. You've got to get those *things* under control. You know Mom isn't going to help. Might as well get your sidekick to do it."

"What do you know about any of this?" I ask.

"Do you listen to anything I say?" Brendan slumps a little lower in my beanbag. "I was at your last meet. Those team swimsuits are thin. You need to double suit like flygirl there." He nods to Nadine. "And, that was the longest, most boring race I've ever seen. I mean, after three laps I lost interest." Brendan pauses. "When you climbed out of the water, you had no secrets."

I hate it when Brendan has a point. So, I refuse to agree. The last thing I need is Brendan feeling superior. I know there must be something wrong with me, but I act like I don't care.

Brendan stands, blows on his fingernails, and buffs them on his shirt. "I'm so good-looking, I put you both to shame. Now, get this done before the new school year. My work here's finished. Ta-ta, girls." With a wave, Brendan is gone.

I close my door.

"Your face is way red," Nadine says.

"My brother was talking about seeing through my swimsuit. Wouldn't you be embarrassed?" *Who else was at the swim meet? Was Golden Boy there? I bet he doesn't even know I'm a swimmer.*

Nadine frowns. "When Dad deploys, it's only girls at home. There isn't much to be embarrassed about."

"Sorry, I forgot about your dad being gone."

Nadine shakes her head. "Let's get back to bra shopping. Hand me your phone."

"What are you going to do?" I hand it over tentatively.

"I'm going to take 'Before and After' pictures so you can see the difference. Now, strike a pose so we can compare it to the after photo."

I put my hands on my hips, one foot forward, and stare at the ceiling. "Do I look smart?"

Nadine imitates a photographer snapping pictures. "Brilliant, darling. Simply dazzling."

There's a movement on the driveway in front of my bedroom window. I glance outside. My parental warning system isn't working today. Did the garage door open? No, that's Talia's car, Mom's co-worker. Did she drop Mom off at the front door? How long ago? Is Mom already in the house? The muscle under my left eye begins to twitch. I know crazy's about to happen. The twitch says, "Pay attention, be ready, and don't drop your guard."

"Nadine, stop." I reach for my phone, but it's too late.

My door opens and Mom steps in. "What are you two

doing? Why's the door closed?"

"Nothing. We're planning a shopping trip," I explain from behind Nadine.

"No." Mom steps up to Nadine. "You're taking pictures of her. Are you sexting?"

"No, ma'am," Nadine responds. "We're pretending to model for a photographer."

"Give me that." Mom pulls my phone out of Nadine's hand and glances at the screen. She moves past Nadine and holds the phone out to me. "How do you unlock this?"

Nadine must have pressed the side button. "Mom, this is crazy. We weren't sexting. That makes no sense."

"You think I'm crazy?" Mom squints. "Am I crazy to pay for this phone? You're lucky to have a phone. *You* should show more respect."

Mom's voice carries her alcohol-heavy breath to my nose. When or where did she drink? Can Nadine smell the liquor too?

"Mom, I don't think you're crazy, only the situation."

I nod toward the door and attempt to telepathically send the words, "Get out, save yourself." It works and Nadine slips out of the room.

"I'm going to keep this." Mom shakes my phone at me. "When your father gets home, I'll show him your filthy pictures. Let's see what happens then. Do you think your father wants to pay the bills for a daughter who's a slut? You could end up homeless on the streets."

"Mom, I'll show you the pictures. They're not filthy." I reach for the phone.

"No, no, no. You're a liar *and* a slut."

I stare at her and will my mouth to stay shut. In my mind, I scream... *A mother shouldn't say that! You can't make me cry.*

She breaks eye contact first, turns, and marches out of the room.

I check for Nadine and am relieved she's gone. Looking in the mirror, my face is red hot. The tears don't show but I feel them wanting to fall. I speak to the reflective surface, "If I don't want to see myself naked, I'm definitely not sexting. I'm not a slut. But I do talk to myself. Does that mean I'm crazy?" Mom's at least... unstable... and I don't want to be like her.

Without my phone, I can't check in with Nadine. E-mail? Mom's probably guarding our one-and-only computer. I tiptoe out of my room and peek into the kitchen. Mom's pouring bourbon into her tumbler. She holds the bottle up to the light, turns to the sink, and adds some water. Ahh, so Dad's marking the bourbon bottle. Who's the liar now?

Mom moves into the living room and sits in front of the television. She clicks on the news, takes a drink, and places the tumbler on the computer desk.

I return to my room and fall onto my bed, my head flopping between the bed and the wall. On the floor is the heating vent and within the dusty grate I see the outline of a small metal ball—a steely. It brings back a sharp memory, to age ten when I first knew Mom didn't like me. I've always known I wasn't perfect enough for her but that was the same day I realized I couldn't tell anyone about... my big momma lie.

It was the end of fourth grade, and I didn't have any friends, except Nadine Thomas. She was the only person who accepted me for who I was. Nadine didn't make fun of my short haircut or say I was more boy than girl. It was nice to have one person on my side, but I didn't really pay attention to what others said about me. I was too busy making enemies by beating everyone at marbles. Other kids played Pokémon cards or other games, but my parents wouldn't spend money on "frivolous" toys. The marbles had been a present from PaPa Gurke, and I had convinced other kids at school to get their own. Each day I would come home with my winnings—their marbles—and watch Sara Jay on the weather channel. Sara obsessed over weather words, and she was always happy. Bad weather made her even happier. The science nerd in me wanted to be her friend.

The day I stopped playing marbles, our electricity was out. I couldn't watch television. I tried to imagine the weather idioms Sara Jay might use to describe my situation.

"Storm's a-brewing. This is a big one, California. The rain has been falling for days, and you know when it rains, it pours. Hundreds of homes are without power. Mudslides have closed all major tunnels around the Bay Area. So, batten down the hatches."

"Why are you such an annoying brat?" my mother said as she walked into the family room, the ever-present glass of brown liquid in hand.

I switched the channel in my head and considered how I might report the situation. *Stay where you are and avoid Linn's house, because this is a shit storm.* In my imaginary weather studio, there was a large map marking my location with a poop emoji.

The pressure in our house had been building for days. Lightning was striking all around us. The air carried the smell of blown transformers and musty dirt under the doors. With every bolt of lightning, Mom's irrationality grew.

"The district meeting isn't important enough to waste your father's time. Why isn't he home?" Mom asked no one in particular for the third time.

Reporter Linn would have said, *Three sheets to the wind.*

Brendan attempted a reasonable answer, "Maybe there's another mudslide. The tunnels are always blocked when it rains this much."

I stayed silent. I recognized the signs, and I knew talking wouldn't work.

"He's never here when the electricity goes out," Mom slurred. "Why do I have to be stuck here with two shitty kids?"

I sent a silent plea to my brother—*Don't answer. Please don't answer.*

"We didn't cause the weather, Mom. You're being ridiculous." Brendan was missing or ignoring my psychic messages.

Mom attempted to focus her bleary eyes on us. "Wait until your father gets home. Then you'll be sorry."

Now, how many times had I heard that drunken threat?

I wanted to add, "Come hell or high water." For once I kept the words to myself.

"How's he going to find us in the dark?" Crap, those words had slipped out. My mouth was operating without permission from my brain.

"You think your father won't paddle you both? I'll make sure of it." Mom's voice had reached the screech level. The house didn't seem large enough for her. She was pacing around the room. Not finding anything useful, Mom grabbed a plastic coaster from the side table and threw it at the wall. Brendan and I ran into my bedroom before she could find something heavier. We should have gotten under the bed, but we made the mistake of jumping on top. Mom was right behind us in full cyclone mode. Fueled by her drunken rage, she looked around for a weapon and grabbed my bag of marbles. She opened the pouch and began to throw them at us.

Despite the lack of electricity, I saw every marble flying toward us as if in slow motion. A handful of glass marbles arced through the air. They reflected the lightning right before they hit our skin. The clear cat's eyes would have been invisible if it weren't for the flash of color in the middle that gave them their name. *This isn't bad*, I told myself. *A few marbles aren't going break anyt— Oh crap, I forgot about the large boulders, they hurt.* A boulder hit my forehead and I realized Brendan had been smarter. He had situated himself next to the wall with me as a bumper. *Thanks, Bro.*

The steelies looked like tiny ghosts. Their gray color cloaked their path, but I knew when one hit the arm I was using to defend my face. Those suckers hurt like the ball bearings they were. I tried to track and dodge the projectiles. My cheek burned when it took a major blow. I recognized the heft of my prize steel boulder. *Why do I own anything so heavy?* I wondered. *That's it; I will never play marbles again.*

Brendan and I covered our faces with our hands and tried to scoot lower on the bed. We knew better than to cry out, though I couldn't keep the tears from streaming down my face.

Mom finally reached the bottom of my marble bag. "Clean up this mess." She threw the leather sack and left the room. It landed on the bed, reminding us how limp our defense against Mom had been.

Brendan and I crawled around in the dark looking for my scattered marbles.

"Geez, how many marbles do you have?" Brendan hissed.

"Two hundred thirty-two regular marbles and ten boulders, approximately."

"Why can't you be a normal girl and play with soft things?"

"I won't get any more marbles, I promise. I'm switching to baseball cards tomorrow."

We found about half of the marbles. Some of the smaller steelies had rolled into the heating vents in the floor. We couldn't reach those. The others were probably hiding in the corner with my pile of clothes. I decided to pick those up when the electricity came back on.

After about thirty minutes of pretending to clean, I heard the front door open. I held my breath until Mom greeted Dad sweetly, "George, how was your day? Did the electrical outage cause you any problems on your drive home?"

Beware, Dad, she's been drinking. It's not safe in this house.

I am amazed at Mom's ability to change personalities when Dad walks through the door. I imagined she must be thinking, *Look at me. I'm so helpful. I haven't been blaming you all day for the storm, the electricity, or the act of procreation. I'm a sweet little wife awaiting my chance to help you during your time of need.*

That was absolutely gag-worthy.

"A mudslide blocked the Caldecott Tunnel. I had to drive around the San Pablo Reservoir. Water was rushing down the canyons and onto the streets. I hydroplaned twice and barely stayed on the road."

I could hear the exhaustion in Dad's voice.

"How about you? I hope there wasn't anything worse than the power being out here?"

"Everything's fine, just perfect. With the electricity out, I can't cook much but I can make you a sandwich. Sit down and I'll take care of everything." Mom's voice was dripping with kindness. She didn't sound normal. And there was no sandwich for Brendan or me.

I blurted out my follow-up weather report. "The cleanup has taken days. Thousands were without power and the roads blocked. The state emergency coalition had every worker on twenty-four-hour shifts. But the real hero was Bella. Amid the largest shit storm this century, she made a sandwich and fluffed a pillow. I'm personally

15

blown away."

"Don't be such a spaz," Brendan said as he listened at the door.

Dad lit candles and placed them on the table. The soft flickering glow convinced Brendan and me to enter the living room. We judged each step as if the ground might shift at any minute. I was glad Dad couldn't see the welts on my face and arms.

"What were you two doing during the storm?" he asked us.

"Not much." Brendan snuck a peek at Mom.

Even without seeing her face, I knew Mom didn't care about Brendan and me. She was only focused on Dad and his opinion of her. Of course, Brendan and I were not supposed to tell Dad what had happened. If we did, she would make us suffer more than marble welts. So, when Dad turned to me, I told my big momma lie, "Everything's fine, just perfect." I used Mom's words to define the truth.

Yes, I lied but I also knew that I had changed. My mother was not going to take marbles away from me. I was in control of what I would do and who I would be. I told Dad everything was fine but what I meant was: I will be fine.

* * *

Dad studies me over the leftovers Mom warmed up and put on the table. "Your mother tells me there was a problem today."

Pushing mushy pasta around my plate has not stopped this moment from coming. Most people who meet my father describe him as intimidating, but he's a marshmallow compared to my mom. *Be careful, Linn. Don't answer too honestly with Mom sitting right here.*

"No problem. Nadine and I were planning a shopping trip. She took a picture of me and Mom misunderstood."

"Look at the pictures," Mom snaps. "Your daughter's

a slut."

Brendan spews his water back into his glass. "Slut? Linn?"

"Brendan," Dad's voice is low, "this discussion is for Linn. Stay out of it."

"Yes, sir." Brendan coughs the word, "fa-uck."

Dad puts the phone on the table. "Unlock it and show me the pictures."

"Dad, I wasn't sexting. Don't you trust me?" I hand the unlocked phone back to him. He scrolls through the pictures and looks at Mom.

"Bella," he asks Mom, "do you want to see these for yourself?"

"So she can liar?" Mom slurs.

Liar? How much bourbon has she drunk?

Dad studies Mom and I can see him make up his mind. Siding with her is more important than the truth. "I'm going to keep this, for now. We'll talk about privileges later."

I should keep my mouth shut but I can't. "You saw there's no dirty pictures and I'm still punished?" Dad doesn't respond. I push my chair back. "Can I be excused? I need to study for finals."

On television, teens cry and stomp into their rooms. But this is my life. Tears cause Dad to ask if I need a reason to cry. When I was young that meant getting spanked. Now, Dad thinks of a worse punishment—yard work on a hot day is his favorite. I try not to react at all. No tears, no stomping, and no begging means it doesn't matter to me. This is survival.

"Yes," Dad says. "You'll be busy with the end-of-year tests. You don't need a phone."

As I stand up, Brendan mouths the question, "Slut?" I shake my head and escape before I start screaming.

Soon, I'll have to ask Dad for money to buy bras. Completely embarrassing! It's like having a loaded wallet pointed at my head—don't move or I'll kill everything you want. I need to grow up and make my own money.

* * *

Journal Entry – Juvenescence at 13

MY TRUTH
Mom doesn't like me. That's not news—I've known this for years. Aren't moms supposed to love you no matter what? What's wrong with me? NO! What's wrong with her?

Dad has my phone. We talked privileges... I'm lucky... Most kids... Their money... Blah, blah, blah. Don't call your mother crazy...

Still, my phone is in his pocket. I don't know when I'll get it back. I need out! Where can a thirteen-and-a-half-year-old swim girl go? Can I swim to Hawaii? Might be worth the effort.

GROWING UP
I don't want to be called names again especially not by my mother. So, I searched for the magazines I got when Grandma Rose bought me a subscription. They're hidden under my bed, covered in dust. Valley Girl Magazine had articles about growing up. They aren't quizzes. I hate quizzes about what character you'd be in some movie or quizzes that tell you if you're a good girlfriend. Who cares? Movies aren't real and I'm not dating so—no. My parents don't believe I wasn't sexting and don't believe I'm

not a slut. I do tell lies, but doesn't everyone? Even if I can't tell the whole truth, shouldn't parents still be helpful? Especially about growing up?

Thank you, VG for the (extremely long) articles. I looked at these a year ago but it didn't mean anything. I'll re-read them all (eventually). I did start summarizing the first one. And, I've been planning. Who needs a mother anyway?

Linn's ~~Grownup~~ Emerging Adult ~~List~~ Plan (LEAP)

1. Growth spurt

— 3 inches in 1 to 2 years ✓

2. Body development (wish I had less) ✓✓

3. Start period—Nope!

Wow! I'm nearly done and I wasn't even trying. Wish I could go back in time and be a child forever. This part of being a girl sucks! I hope I never have a period, period. Why don't boys have periods?

Read most of the next article—Personal and Emotional Development. Hoping to find out why I have to grow up. No answers but I found something I want to try.

<u>4. BE SELF-SUFFICIENT</u>

I'm sure this means getting a driver's license. If I drive, I could get a job, and get out of the house. Something that pays more than babysitting. Be independent! Note to self— check the internet to see how old you have to be to start driving. In the meantime, I'll start a 'my growing up' plan. My 'I don't need a mother' plan.

Start with LEAP 4, Becoming self-sufficient.

Linn

Walker

Gurke

Chapter 2
Well-Rounded Loser

I'VE BEEN PRETEND-STUDYING for a week now. It's like writing notes in class. My science book is on my desk turned to an important page. I have a pad and pencil, with some real notes, sitting next to me. At school, I have to make eye contact with the teacher occasionally and look thoughtful. At home, I need to seem focused on "studying." Today, I have one of the Valley Girl articles nearby. When I hear footsteps, I slide the textbook over the words I'm reading and pull my eyebrows together. I'm going for the science-is-so-difficult face.

"Stop sexting." Brendan walks into my room.

My head snaps up from my not-studying text. "You stop! I wasn't sexting, and you know it." Even I'm surprised by how angry I sound. "What do you want, Brendan?"

Brendan stops inside the room and tilts his head. He concentrates on the music coming from the CD playing on my old boom box. "Why are you listening to an angry girl band?"

"I like their songs."

"I don't see you as the angry type."

I glare at Brendan. "You'll change your mind when I beat the crap out of you."

"I'm too fast. You'll never catch me."

I let out a sigh. "Why are you here, Brendan?"

"You've got mail." He waves an envelope around. "This was sitting on the front porch." He steps up next to my desk holding the package far enough away that I have to reach to grab it.

"It's from MeMe and PaPa Gurke in Oregon," I announce.

"I know, I can read." He continues to stand next to me.

I recognize Brendan's curiosity and decide to push my advantage. "Thanks," I say and put the envelope on my desk unopened.

"Open it, Spaz. I want to see what our grandparents sent you and not me."

I grab a pencil from my desk and work it under the flap.

"Could you go any slower?" Brendan complains.

"Yep." I pull up and the seal rips open. I dump a thin box onto the desk and give the envelope another tap—empty.

"Oh, lookie." Brendan laughs. "You got a box—you're special."

I wave it around. "They did send me a gift."

"Yeah, MeMe has sent me two of those. It's a pen made at PaPa's factory."

I open the box to see if he's right. "The pen's made of Myrtlewood." I'm good at facts.

"Yeah, yeah, what does the post-it say?"

I glance at the note. "Happy eighth-grade graduation."

"They won't be coming."

I frown at Brendan. "Who? Coming where?"

"MeMe and PaPa," he responds. "Don't get excited. They won't be at your graduation."

"I wasn't excited. MeMe always kisses me. She uses too much perfume and has lady whiskers. It creeps me out."

Brendan shakes his head. "You've got to grow a brain."

"What does that mean?"

"How long has she planted wet ones on you?" Brendan tilts his head. "Long enough for you to learn—stay out of her reach. You never see her grabbing me. Do you?"

Jerking Brendan's vanity chain is too easy. "No, because she likes me more."

"Duh, the rela-freaks prefer you. People hang with their own kind."

"Rela-freaks?"

"Relatives from the shallow end of the gene pool. Geeks, mutants, and weirdos like you."

"Not like you?"

"Nope. I'm way too awesome for Dad's family... and don't get me started on Mom's inbreeds. The hospital switched me at birth. My real parents were intelligent, beautiful—"

Can you hurt yourself by rolling your eyes too much?

I cut off Brendan's fantasy. "What does it take to get your driver's license?"

Brendan shakes his head. "You can't drive. You're not old enough."

"I'll be fourteen in September. I want to be self-sufficient, which means driving."

Brendan laughs. "Self-sufficient... that's rich. All I do is run errands and drive your sorry ass around."

"Seriously, how do I get my license?"

"Get older, take a class, do a butt-load of practice hours, and pass a test. It sounds easy, but it's a lot more complicated. Remind me to introduce you to the internet."

"I've already downloaded an instruction booklet. I know I'm too young to drive, but there's lots more to do before you actually drive. I was talking about getting Mom and Dad to let me get a license."

Brendan belly laughs until he's near tears. He fans himself. "I can't wait. Let me know when you plan to tell them. I want to watch."

"You did it," I grumble. "It's only fair for me to get a license too."

"Keep dreaming, smart one." Brendan taps my head

with his knuckles. "Before you can drive, you have to pass those tests you're—" Brendan flips my science book closed "—not studying for." He snorts. "I know all the tricks, Dipwad. I created the not-really-studying one."

"Of course you did," I respond with another eye roll.

"Enjoy your... pen." Brendan turns and walks out.

I wait until I hear his footsteps fade away to inspect my gift and talk to it like a new friend. "I'll name you Myrtle 'cause you're made of Myrtlewood. Probably bought at cost... I'm so special."

Most pens are a problem for leftys. Teachers say we don't hold them correctly, well I say it's correct. Still the ink gets smeared when I write. This one must have quick drying ink 'cause it doesn't smear. That's good news! Myrtle has a lighthouse etched on it. In all our visits to Coos Bay, I've never visited any lighthouse. That's not good or bad news, just a fact.

* * *

Staring at my mirror, I visualize myself as the sheriff in an old western movie. I shine my make-believe badge. "I ain't talking 'bout money. This here's 'bout growing up." Sheriff Linn tips her imaginary hat and struts out of my room.

By the time I reach the family room, most of my bravado's gone. "Dad?" I wait until he looks up from the book he's reading. "I need to sign up for driver's ed this summer. They only take credit cards. Can I use yours?"

"No, Linn, you *want* to take driver's education. You don't *need* it. You only need air, water, food, clothing, and shelter. Your mother and I pay for your basic needs. But you need to work for what you want. There is some question about shelter and clothing. Are those last two needed or are they a privilege?" Dad waits.

Arggg, were gunslingers this concerned with preci-

sion in their speech? How to answer his question without screaming? "I think shelter and clothing are needs," I say as calmly as I can.

"Yes, but only the basics. We don't have to provide a nice house or buy you new clothes. Anything that keeps you dry and warm is enough."

"But... about the license, I don't *need* driver's ed. I appreciate the advantages you and Mom provide our family. Still, I'd like to add a license to my list of privileges. To take one of those classes I'm required to sign up online and pay with a credit card. May I use yours?" I slowly take a deep breath to recover without Dad seeing my frustration. *Speaking logically is exhausting!*

"You have to be fourteen to take driver's education." Dad attempts to read his book.

"I'll be fourteen in September," I announce.

Dad furrows his brow. "You can't be. You're still finishing eighth grade."

"I turned thirteen last September, Dad."

"And you'll turn fourteen this year?"

I try not to tell him that's how time works, but I can't stop my eyes from rolling. "Yes, in a few months. Can I please use your credit card?"

"No," Dad declares quickly.

Is he listening at all? I ball my fists and tell myself that hitting my father would be a bad idea. Slowly I make my hands relax. "Why not?"

Dad raises one finger. "You're still too young. You can't even get the permit until you're at least fifteen and a half. Come back next summer when you're almost fifteen and we'll discuss how much the class you *want* costs."

I turn and walk back toward my room, completely broken. Dad's loaded wallet took me down without leaving his pocket. If I were a gunslinger or sheriff, the undertaker would be measuring me for a pine box.

And still no phone. I'm really beginning to hate that computer in the living room.

* * *

I hear footsteps coming toward my room. I arrange my face into what I hope is a normal, not-upset-about-the-driving-class expression.

"Linn..." Dad stops at my door and stares. "You okay?" *I guess I don't look normal.* Dad shrugs and places a box with a large trash bag on the floor. "We're having a garage sale Saturday. Please go through your room and fill this box with things you want to sell."

"Why are we doing a garage sale?" I sit up and lean forward. "We're not moving again, are we? I mean, I haven't even started high school yet. There are so many things I plan—"

"Stop." Dad puts his hands up. "Why do you and your brother jump to negative conclusions about everything? We want to clean up and make room for... next year."

"Why do we need to make room?" My voice sounds childish.

Dad pinches his nose. "Can you do this? Fill the box? If you help with the sale on Saturday, you can keep the money your items bring in."

The thought of cash makes the garage sale sound reasonable. "How much can I charge?"

"Fill the box." Dad turns and walks away mumbling about his greedy kids.

I sit on the floor in front of my closet. The collection of Barbies and one Ken doll is the first things I see. *I haven't played with these for at least a year.* I place all but my two favorites in the box. I can't get rid of swim Barbie or teacher Barbie.

An hour later my box is full. Besides the dolls, I've added a random troll, a few electronic games, and a lot of stuffed animals. Also the bag of marbles that I found buried in the back of my closet. I'm not going to bother with the ones still in the heating vent. I'm keeping the collection of Beanie Babies, mature or not.

I start to reorganize my closet. In the back corner is a pile of shoe boxes. I pull them forward and begin putting the empties in the trash bag. "If I find ten empty boxes, I'm officially a hoarder," I announce to my room. "Am I obsessive if I open each one hoping to find something?" I look up into my mirror but there's no response. I take the lid off box number eight and freeze. The memory hits me hard. I close my eyes and hold my breath. *I wore a brace with this shoe when I was four. When did it start? And how have I forgotten it already?*

I can still feel the heavy plastic around my right knee and down my leg. I've never forgotten how it weighed me down and ruined only one shoe. *Did I stop remembering because it makes me sad?* I pick up the shoe. "Why are you here?" Shoving the shoe and box back into the corner of my closet, I go to find Dad in the garage.

"Dad, I remember I wore a leg brace when I was young. I don't need it anymore, right?"

"Obviously. You haven't worn that brace for years now. Why are you asking?"

"I found my worn shoe. Why haven't we talked about my brace ever?"

"We didn't need to talk about it. You're fine now. You were born with a twisted right knee. When you started to walk, you stepped with your left foot and then placed your right foot on the left and fell down. Your right knee is still twisted. You walk normally because the brace shifted your lower leg. Now you don't step on your own foot." Dad chuckles, "You bruised your forehead so often, we told people you were sprouting horns."

"Great," I respond. "I probably have brain damage."

"It could've happened," he jokes. "When we were too broke to afford a movie, we would take your brace off and watch you attempt to walk. It was hilarious."

"Making fun of a disabled child." I cross my arms and sit in a folding chair.

"I'm joking, Linn. Calm down. Your knee wasn't a disability. It was an obstacle, a challenge, a problem to solve. It taught you to get back up and try again. Your stubborn streak is forty to sixty percent genetic; I blame your mother." Dad smiles. "Wearing the brace made you try harder to walk. I'm proud of you for not giving up."

Compliments make my eyes sting. *Is this the same guy who took my phone for not sexting?* I don't understand. *Do you care about me, Dad?* I keep my focus on the table in front of me. "Why do you always side with Mom?"

There's a long pause before he speaks. "I don't take sides, Linn. I love all my family, equally." His voice is low, and his words are measured.

"I wasn't sexting and I'm not a slut. And I should get my phone back."

"Of course. You're a good kid."

"Then why didn't you tell Mom she was wrong?"

"You have to understand how much your mother suffers. Your Grandfather Jed was a cruel man. He taught your mother she'd become an evil temptress as she grew up. Bella's trying to move beyond his teachings, but it's difficult. There's no point arguing with her. I try to show her alternative views so she can live a happy life. You should do the same."

"What about the alcohol?"

"She doesn't drink that much." Dad's voice is tight. "It might hit her a little harder because she's so thin now. Let's not mention this again. Your mother idolized her father and won't listen to any criticism of him."

I sit and fume when Dad walks back into the house.

Keep your mouth shut, Linn. Forget the truth, Linn. Pretend everything's fine, Linn. Lie, Linn!

* * *

"Mirror, mirror on my door, oh what am I here for?" I cringe at my joke. "What? No response?" *It's suburbia, there's no royalty, no magic, no nothing, and definitely no talking mirrors. Even if the mirror spoke, it would tell me Brendan's better looking.*

Today's only the third time this year I've seen my reflection. Correction, I don't think I've stood here more than four times in my life. Dad's right. My left knee points straight ahead. The other is... I'm not sure what you call that direction. Off? Twisted? Is this why Mom doesn't like me? *I don't care what she thinks, I'm fine. Maybe.*

"Geez, Linn, you'll break the mirror. You don't need bad luck."

"Brendan, get out of my room."

"An open door's an invitation, Idjit. Dad said to get you for dinner."

"If only I could be an only child," I reply.

Brendan laughs. "You'd be bored without me."

I follow Brendan out and sit in my regular chair at the dinner table. *I don't want to admit it, but he's right.*

"What did you learn today, Linn?"

Mom's channeling her good mother personality and I make the mistake of being honest.

"Dad explained why I wore a brace when I was little. He said it made me stronger."

Mom drops her fork onto her plate. "There's nothing wrong with either of my children." She gives Dad a tight-lipped smile. "Your father doesn't remember much. It was a little issue, we helped you and everything's perfect now." Mom's upper lip begins to curl as she attempts to hide the lie and put a smile on her face.

"Everything's perfect?" Dad repeats. "Do you hear yourself? You sound like your sister."

Mom pops up, knocks her chair over, and points at me. The good mother personality is gone. "You've ruined another meal. I hope you're happy." She grabs her tumbler and charges toward the back of the house.

"It's my fault." Dad apologizes and stands. "I'll see if I can fix this."

Once Dad leaves, I turn to Brendan. "I ruined dinner? What did I do wrong?"

"You want to drive, and you don't know anything." Brendan continues eating. "You cut into Mom's blind spot, her perfection lane." Brendan shakes his head. "When are you going to learn? Driving's like life—watch the others around you and expect crazy. Signal to enter another person's lane. Be ready to stay put if they seem unstable. It's the only way to survive."

I sit at the table, speechless. The mirror doesn't lie. I'm a twisted-knee girl. *I need—not want—to be self-sufficient so I can get out of this house.* Changing my name to 'Fault-line Linn.' When Fault-line Linn enters a room, the earth begins to shake.

Brendan gestures at me. "Pass the ketchup, Spaz. This meatloaf needs help."

* * *

Journal Entry – Middle School's Over

I cleaned the toys out of my closet to make room for adulthood. See how mature I am? Nadine and I made a plan to just have her show up on Sunday to take me bra shopping. I didn't bother to tell my parents. I mean, they don't tell me everything, either. Mom and Dad couldn't say no when Mrs. Thomas and Nadine showed up at our door. Then I asked Dad for money. That was fun—not! But I didn't want to spend what little I'd made at the garage sale. We then hit the sales. Mostly I stuck with white bras, but Nadine talked me into the purple sports bra. (Okay, it didn't take much talking. I really like that purple bra.)

I didn't talk about the shopping trip with anyone else. Mom doesn't care and Dad doesn't want to talk about girl stuff. I think he wishes I was a boy.

Middle school is over and I'm going to be in high school soon. But I'm not old enough to get my driving license. I Googled it and started a to-do list. Show identification, prove address, pay a fee, pass written and eye tests, take a class, blah, blah, blah. It was page twelve before the age thing came up. Fourteen isn't old enough for the permit or the class. The website makes me feel like growing up is wrong or at the very least too expensive. I'll be a high school loser.

LEAP
I was working on LEAP 4, Being self-sufficient. When I asked Brendan about my driver's license, he laughed. Brendan doesn't take me seriously, but that's not new. Can I be self-sufficient without driving? I made money at the garage sale—almost ten dollars. It's a start to becoming self-sufficient—whatever that means.

I read more of the Valley Girl article about Personal and Emotional Development. Using my new pen, I added another task to my list.

<u>5. DATING AND PREFERENCE</u>
I know my preference but I'm not dating. Why do people think preference is a choice? I didn't make a choice. With Golden Boy hanging around our house, I'm interested. Just not interested in Steve! Not sure when this happens to others. I don't remember waking up one day and thinking... boys or girls? Some people get confused by what they see and hear from their parents but, not me. I shouldn't complain, but the article didn't talk about sex. I don't know who wrote the article, but sex must be part of dating and preference. I need to know how long you should date before having sex and how it happens (I don't know who I can ask).

Even with my LEAP List, I'm confused about what it means to grow up. It can't be as simple as selling your toys out of the garage. Or even being able to drive.

This would be easier if I could trust my parents. Aren't they supposed to be helping?

Linn

Walker

Gurke

Chapter 3
The Brendan Flex

I BOLT UPRIGHT WHEN Mom opens my bedroom door. "Get up," she says, "it's Monday."

Oh crap. I glance at the alarm clock as she walks out of my room. *Am I late for school?* "Wait, it's summer." I slump back under the covers. "High School Orientation," I groan and roll out of bed. I sniff the jeans and t-shirt hanging on the chair—*good enough for one more day.* I pull the brush through my hair, smear my face with SPF lotion, and hurry out.

When I see the cereal boxes on the table in front of Mom, I'm glad I'm running late. "I'll grab a slice of bread and some milk."

"Don't take my good glasses. Use a travel cup, you can't break those."

I rush through the kitchen and head toward the sound of a honking horn. As I exit the house, I glance around for neighbors. *It's not like Dad doesn't know neighbors will object to early morning noise.*

"You awake?" Dad asks me as I buckle up.

"Um, yeah."

"You've never been a morning person." Dad laughs. "When you were a baby, I'd check each morning to see if you were breathing. What baby sleeps pasts nine?"

"Me." I attempt a real conversation. "Did you have a good Father's Day last week?"

"Excellent. I got to watch the entire Giants game. The

33

Father's Day games are always great. Some of the players bring their dads to the stadium and others bring their children. The game was full of great father-son stories from both teams. And the Giants won."

"The hamburgers Brendan grilled were good."

"Yes! Served with your mother's homemade bread, they were spectacular burgers." Dad glances at me. "I also enjoyed your guacamole. You're becoming a good cook."

I roll my eyes. "I cut and mixed avocados with some salsa that was in the fridge. Not sure that's the same as cooking."

"In my book it is."

"Uh, Dad?" I look at him more closely. "Why're you wearing work clothes?"

"School starts in a few weeks. I'm a principal, Linn, I've told you this. Administrators, teacher representatives, and student leaders will be available today. A school doesn't open by itself. I'm going to drop you off and head to my campus. We're also holding an orientation."

"So, how will I get home?"

"Brendan's at the Student Council table. He'll give you a ride."

Dad pulls into the parking lot and stops near the walkway. "You're a little early, but it's better than being late." He reaches into his jacket pocket and hands me my phone. "You're going to need this today, but don't do anything foolish."

"I never have." *Does he think I'm going to sext in public?* Still, I had waited him out.

As soon as Dad drives away, I check my contact list on Snapchat. I'm such a loser, I only have Nadine listed as a friend. She has left a bunch of messages. They all say pretty much the same thing.

NADINE: Thinking of you what's

going on with your mom? trust me

NADINE: Are you there? still no phone???

NADINE: See you at orientation

I type a quick response.
ME: Got my phone back
everything's fine see you soon

I walk toward what I hope is the center of the buildings.

After passing a couple of buildings, I find myself in a large open area with tables set up at the edges. I study the options for academic groups and athletics. Dad was right when he said I was early. There are only a few students talking to those sitting at the tables. Each table has a poster with the name of the organization. No sign of Nadine but Brendan's sitting behind the Student Council sign talking to a couple of girls. I walk over and line up behind them. Once they leave, I move up.

"Welcome to The Burn," Brendan recites while reading a Student Council application.

"What's The Burn?" I ask.

Brendan's head pops up. He checks to see if anyone's around. "What're you doing here?"

"Same thing you're doing, orientation. Remember? I'll be a student here. Shouldn't you give me the Student Council pitch? I might want to run for office."

"No." Brendan lowers his voice. "This is my thing. You're... *not* to coattail me."

"Coattail?" I ask. "How do you, coattail someone?"

"Don't copy me. I'm known for student government. You need to do your own thing. You're already involved with band and swimming. You can do anything else you want as long as it isn't what I do. Go check the Key Club two tables over. They're all nerds like you."

"Okay, but I need a ride home. Should I meet you back here?"

"No. Wait until everyone's gone and sit over there." Brendan points to an empty table in the middle. "Now go find a nerd group to join."

"I will make it so," I say in my best Star Trek voice. "But you never told me, what's The Burn?"

"This school, Spaz. Don't you listen to anything? I've told you this a zillion times."

"You mean Firestorm High, right?"

"Why do you have to be so literal? Yes, Firestorm. Most of us call it The Burn, Scorched Earth, or Combustion Junction. It's a simile."

"But a simile is a comparison of two things. What's the school compared to?"

"Thanks, Smarty-Pants. Now go."

"I don't think you should joke about fire."

"Tell that to the idiots who named the school after a natural disaster." Brendan shakes his head and looks back at his paper. Clearly, this discussion is over.

I move toward the Key Club table and line up behind the same two girls that were at Brendan's station earlier. It takes me a minute to realize one of the girls is talking to me.

"Are you Brendan's sister?"

I focus on the girls and try to wish them away, but they don't move. "Yes."

"I thought I saw you shopping with him. My name's Sue, I work at the grocery store."

"Hi, I'm Linn."

"Your brother's hot," Sue's friend gushes. "I love his haircut and blue eyes. Is he seeing anyone? Does he like girls or boys?"

"I don't know, you should ask him." I'm not interested

in discussing Brendan's love life.

"Are you really his sister?" the giddy girl asks.

"Yes." I'm losing my patience with Sue's minion. "His no-so-hot sister." I make a point of searching behind me. I'm hoping for Nadine... or anyone else.

"Come on, let's check out the dance team." Sue moves her friend away.

When they step away, I stare at... WOW. A-mazing guy... copper skin, brown eyes, dimpled chin, and hair. Yep, he has hair... *What's wrong with me? Stop overthinking and focus on, WOW.*

"He's hot." Wow Boy mocks the dippy girl's gush. "Those blue eyes, ohhh."

Shut your mouth, Linn, don't drool.

He extends his hand. "Hi, I'm Alan. Sorry, but I was listening to your conversation."

I take his outstretched hand. "Are those rings?" I'm studying his jewelry. "Sorry. I'm not trying to be creepy. I've never seen anything like these."

"I make them myself from recycled and natural materials. I collect spoons and candlesticks. You know, shit you find in yard sales. Then I imbed seashells or walnut husks and fire them in a kiln I built. I sell them at craft festivals. You should come to one and help me." Alan holds back a smile. "Bring your ditsy friends who like your brother."

"I get that all the time," I grumble. "Brendan's eyes get a lot of attention. Big deal, they're ice blue. I don't want to answer the other questions. I mean, he's my brother but... we don't talk about real-life stuff."

Alan fidgets with the papers on his table. "I met Brendan last year in tech class. I can tell you, he does like girls." Alan glances at me and reads my how-do-you-know face. "I asked. He seemed pretty chill about my interest in him."

"Okay?" I try not to whine about a guy who prefers my

brother. *I mean, what do you say?*

"Well, now you know." Alan grins at me. "And according to G. I. Joe, that's the battle."

"Half the battle," I correct.

Alan scratches his nose with his middle finger.

I like this guy already—he's funny. "So, are you going to tell me about the Key Club?"

"Sir, yes sir," Alan salutes me, and we both snort.

* * *

By the time I leave Alan's table, I've filled out an application for the Key Club and I have one for Nadine. More students have arrived. I search the crowd for my friend. I wouldn't have noticed Steve Miller except he's acting like a total freshman by waving a piece of paper and pointing to a nearby building. I forgot 'Steve the Dweeb' would be following me to high school. I stand on my tiptoes to see who Steve has cornered. The person is bobbing and weaving in an attempt to escape his attention. I know how *that* feels.

Ah, the hair, Nadine's favorite blowout. It's her in-between look. She says it communicates not willing to dress up but caring enough to put in an effort. For the first time this morning, I realize I haven't put in any effort. I touch my hair and try to remember if I used a brush this morning. I know I got to the SPF lotion. I can feel it melting down my face. *Pretty sure my hair screams a bad attitude. Nothing new.*

I walk over, staying behind Steve so I can surprise Nadine. When I get close enough, I can hear their voices.

"Come on, Nadine." Steve sounds excited. "If you go inside the admin building, they'll give you a schedule. Otherwise, you have to wait for it to be e-mailed."

"So?" Nadine steps to one side and Steve follows for the block.

I want to laugh but I crouch lower to avoid being seen and take a couple of steps forward.

"Don't ya wanta know?" Steve asks.

I can hear Nadine let out a sigh. "I can wait."

I stand up behind Steve. Using my Yoda voice I whisper, "Patience, you must have."

Steve spins around so fast I'm afraid he'll fall over. "Pickle girl!" He throws his arms around me in a way-too-close hug.

My body goes stiff. *I hate when he calls me pickle and I hate being touched.* I lower my voice and attempt to sound calm. "Back away and I won't beat the crap out of you."

Steve drops his arms and takes a step back. He gives me a smile. "You wouldn't actually hurt me. I'm lovable, right? Linn?"

How to respond without knocking the loveable out of Steve?

Nadine grabs my hand. "Come on Linn, let's go find the swim table and sign up."

Nadine steps around Steve and drags me away. "He's not worth the effort it would take to beat him up."

"Sorry," I mumble. "I wasn't trying to be angry. It just happens."

"Don't worry." Nadine points to the area with the tables. "There's the swim club. Now that we're in high school it's getting serious."

I know she's talking to help me feel positive. All I can do is nod. A couple of older swimmers are behind the table, both wearing hoodies in the summer. They were probably in a pool earlier today. Practice pools are kept way too cold.

"Oh good. Here's Nadine," the girl in the black hoodie says. "So glad to see you and... umm, your friend."

"I carry her gym bag." I pretend panic. "I've lost it already."

Hoodie girl looks at Nadine, hoping for help. "We need people to swim the butterfly." She can't make eye contact. "And you... swim?"

"Distance. The 500 freestyle, you know, the one right after you get out of the pool having finished all two laps of your race. Then I do ten laps, basically five times as many." I stare at hoodie girl long enough to see she's blushing. *What's wrong with me today?* "Sorry, I didn't mean to sound like such a jerk. My name's Linn Gurke and I'm your slow and steady swimmer."

"Yes." Hoodie girl turns and rummages through a box. "I remember seeing the name Gurke." She pulls a form out of the box and hands it to me. "We've been expecting you." She seems so happy to have found the information sent from the middle school.

I decide not to tell her we were on the same team for two years. I mean, I don't remember her name either. "Thanks," I mutter and reach for a pen.

Of course, Nadine finishes filling in her application before me. She beats me at everything. We turn away from the swim table and consider the now crowded area. I glance toward the Key Club station but the space in front of Alan is packed.

"I hate to say it," Nadine whispers. "But we should take Steve's advice and get our schedules."

"As long as he's not there when we show up," I murmur in a low voice. Steve and his family moved into the area at the beginning of sixth grade. I put up with his hyperactive foot tapping on my chair all through middle school, and I'm hoping that I don't have any classes with him this year. If anyone's last name had started with an H, I, J, K, or L... pretty much any letter other than T, I wouldn't have had Steve sitting behind me!

We both laugh at our spy voices and head toward the administration building. The lines are short and it doesn't take long to claim our schedules. Outside we grab a bench and compare our classes. *We only share P.E. and lunch— the two times you can socialize. It's something.*

Nadine slaps her schedule on her leg. "We're not going to see each other much."

"There's always swim team and after school. I forgot to tell you I picked up an application for the Key Club for you." I hand over the paperwork.

"Why the Key Club?" Nadine asks.

"Well, I met Alan... he's... a cool guy and he was at the Key Club desk."

"Oh." Nadine pokes me in the ribs. "You're interested."

"No." I think about how to respond without spilling any Alan beans. "He's not my type."

"Is that why you're angry today?"

Nadine's question catches me by surprise. "What?"

"I've been trying to figure it out." Nadine shrugs and gives me a side glance. "You freaked out when Steve grabbed you. Not saying I would welcome a Steve hug, but it seemed a bit much. Then you got angry at the swim table. What's wrong?"

I glance at the ground and think for a minute. "I said in my text earlier, everything's fine." I lie.

Nadine shakes her head. "I keep telling you, trust me." She waits. "When you're ready."

I don't speak. I'm busy thinking of how to protect Nadine and myself at the same time from my mother's behavior.

Nadine stands. "There's Mom. She's dropping the twins at a party. Call me, anytime."

I plaster a smile on my face and wave at Nadine's mother. "I will," I reply as she leaves.

I sit and think about everything Nadine said and why I'm angry. I still don't have any answers when my phone vibrates. I glance down to see a text from Brendan.

BRENDAN: Where are you?

ME: Bench in front of the Admin building

BRENDAN: Stay. I'm coming

I tilt my head up. "Oh goody."

* * *

Brendan's checks the area as he hurries around the corner. "What're you doing here?"

"I've been here all day. Remember? I talked to you earlier."

"That was in the quad. Why are you by the administration building?"

"Nadine and I picked up our schedules. She left right before you texted. Why?"

"Teachers check into this building each morning. Stay away from it."

"Why?"

"If you're in the administration building, it means trouble. I never get in trouble and, you shouldn't either. The principal worked with Dad a couple of years ago. And everyone knows Mom. She's the Kindergarten Queen in this district. You've got to be careful."

"Why?"

"Stop being an Idjit, Linn. You know Mom can't handle her children doing anything wrong. She wants you to be perfect, like me."

"Perfect? Like you?"

"Yes, like me. I never make Mom and Dad look bad. Come on, I'll show you the school." Brendan glances around again. "I know you've been here before. For baseball games and track meets. But you haven't seen the rest of the campus. This year I get to park in the S-Lot over there." Brendan points to the left. "Seniors can have cars at school. It's only right. Our group's the first to make a real difference here. I'm one of the leaders."

I roll my eyes and follow Brendan as he walks toward the first building.

"They built this place as an open campus but didn't think about school shootings. I'm working with the student government to create a security plan. We installed those gates over there."

"The security plan you're creating?" I bat my eyelashes at Brendan. "Wow. What a guy. I hate to tell you, but a gate isn't going to stop school shooters."

"Open campus, Nitwit. Someone could drive a car right up to the classrooms."

"Well, I'll sleep better tonight knowing that Brendan's protecting me with a gate."

"I wasn't working alone. Javy's helping me with the SAFFE Facebook page, and his dad is with the ATF. Mr. Ramos has given me advice about shooters, firearms, and the weaponization of cars."

"Facebook?" I hurry to walk alongside Brendan. *We aren't allowed to use social media. Dad's crazy about keeping our names and pictures off the internet.* "Hello, identity theft and facial recognition software. What are you doing?"

"It's not my Facebook page. It belongs to SAFFE— Student Association For Firestorm Emergencies. It's a synonym, Dipwad. My name is still protected."

"You mean acronym. A synonym has the same or close to—"

"Shut it, Linn." Brendan glances at me. "You seriously don't deserve my efforts. They should strap you to a post with a sign—Take her, leave the smart kids."

Brendan turns and walks to where the tables were this morning. "The outdoor seating in the quad is for the cafeteria. The cafeteria's straight ahead. You can go inside and get your typical slop. Or pack your lunch. The cool kids order from the kiosk at the front and sit outside. I'm one of the cool kids. I sit here." Brendan points to a table.

I breathe deeply. *Eucalyptus. There must be a grove of trees nearby.* "Smells like the spa Nadine goes to. She said the scent's good for you, cures what ails you."

"Tell your Cootie Booty friend to stop wasting her money. Smells here are free."

"Technically, taxes pay for schools."

Brendan waves at the buildings. "Here's something that'll make your nerd heart happy. Each classroom building holds one grade level. You'll have your classes in the freshman building. The vocation building is between you rookies and the sop-mores. The seniors are on the other side of the quad. You'll be as far away as possible from me, and our schedules will never overlap. Except for maybe P.E. There's no need for me to see you. Understand?"

"But you'll drive me to school, right?"

"Most days I can bring you. At the end of the day, you can meet me at the car. When I have after-school stuff, you'll have to line up with the other losers for the yellow menace."

"You rode the bus last year," I point out.

Brendan ignores my comment and returns to his lecture voice. "The teachers here are okay. Ms. Hess is a great English teacher, but she's too serious. Hess tries to get into everyone's life and save the world. She probably spends her weekends defending trees, dolphins, and free-range chickens. You're gonna love her. I had two classes with her and got an A both times."

"You got A's in English? How did you *not* learn about acronyms?"

"I have skills you've never thought of, Bubbles. I'm the real deal. I know teachers because I pay attention to

Mom and Dad. You don't need to know facts if you study teachers."

"Manipulate Ms. Hess, get A's, be awesome like Brendan." I pretend to answer my phone. "Reality? Calling for Brendan? He's not here right now. Try the psych ward."

"Stop, you need to listen and learn how to keep your head down." Brendan stands up and walks toward the side of the cafeteria. "You know the athletic fields are back here. These buildings are open all year. Coach runs a weight-training program in the summer. The athletes come here and prep for the upcoming season."

"You're a sports type. Why aren't you doing weights?" I ask.

"I've already made it to the pole-vaulting finals and I'm not playing baseball this year. I'm good." Brendan flexes his muscles and runs his hands up and down his sides.

I snort. "It's the Brendan flex. Now you want me to believe you're awesome and pumped? Reality check, dude."

Brendan turns on me. "Reality? Again?"

I stumble back a step. His face's redder than I've ever seen it.

"How's that working for you, Linn? Huh? Is reality helping you? Does the truth say you measure up? Eyes wide open, Dumb-Shit, do you feel loved?"

I mutter some stupid noises. I don't remember ever seeing him this mad.

"Yeah, that's what I thought. In case you haven't noticed, our family values are keeping secrets and 'shut the fuck up.' Don't you listen to anything? I'm telling you how to do this. No one told me. I had to figure it out myself. This is how you survive. You tell everyone you're special and keep saying it, keep saying it, keep saying it until you believe it."

Brendan's anger looks like Mom, but then it's gone.

"Brendan," I attempt to control the tears, "you're

special. I thought we were kidding. You don't have to try, you're—"

"Shut it!" Brendan yells.

"Hey, guys. Everything okay here?" A voice comes from behind Brendan.

I peek around Brendan's stiff body. *Oh crap.* Now my face is turning red. "Javy," I announce carefully. "Brendan was showing me around the school."

"Hey, Linn." Javy furrows his brows. "You seem upset."

Brendan works up a smile before he turns to his friend. "I was warning Linn to watch out for narcs."

"At Firestorm?" Javy laughs. "I don't think they do undercover cops in high schools anymore. That's some 80s movies stuff, right there. But, I wouldn't put it past Principal Greene. He's still living in the past."

Act normal, nothing to see here. Keep lying, brush it off. "What are you doing here, Javy?" I ask.

"Coach's motivational techniques." He shrugs. "Every day he has a distance run. I figure if I can keep up with the cross-country team, I'll be ready for soccer season."

Think of something intelligent, this is your chance. Open your mouth—say anything.

"I'm sure you'll outdistance all those joggers," Brendan teases.

"I think the cross-country team is beyond jogging, I think they run."

"Joke, Linn. Geez, you are so lame." Brendan shakes his head. "See ya later, Javy. Gotta take the Idjit home now." We both wave and walk back to the car in silence.

"I'm sorry," I apologize as Brendan pulls the car out of the parking lot.

"Forget it," he mumbles. "Like everything in our lives, pretend it never happened and avoid discussing reality."

"Okay, the quiet game starts now." I lean against the car window and stare at the side mirror. *People in the mir-*

ror are more damaged than they appear.

* * *

Journal Entry – Ready for High School—NOT

I'll never belong in high school. Might as well start the countdown for failure to conform in 10... 9..... I thought Brendan felt good about himself, but he doesn't. I was feeling sorry for myself. Then I saw Brendan's truth. He was angry and... I don't know, broken? Scarred? If you could see the hurt Mom has left on Brendan, his face would be one massive scar.

LEAP
Continue LEAP 5, Dating (anyone?)

I met a ~~gorgeous~~ hot boy—Alan. For a minute I thought he might help my dating situation. But Alan's a no-go. I'm not his type. My guess—is he prefers Brendan. But he's not Brendan's type. I like Golden Boy, but I doubt he knows I exist. Brendan was yelling at me when Golden Boy showed up. But we lied to him. Honestly, being honest is difficult. The whole thing's too confusing to fix. Guess I don't have to worry about sex if nothing's happening.

I read more of the Valley Girl article—Personal and Emotional Development. It says I need to decide who I am. It's really hard to stay awake when you're reading about lobes and shedding. New expectation for my LEAP list...

6. FIND YOUR IDENTITY

Do I have a choice? Or is my identity already written in my jeans/genes—ha! I am hilarious. Seriously, I'm not sure I know what this means. The article makes it sound like I'm old enough to decide who I am... but am I? When was someone going to tell me this?

The article listed things to expect from your parents. Things like communication, honesty, understanding, and support. I don't think these authors have ever met real parents. The last one on the list got me laughing. It said parents should honor and respect your independence. Ha!

Honestly and respectfully, reading the article didn't help me figure out who I am. Maybe identity's a job. Mom and Dad tell people they're teachers as if that word explains everything. I think the word 'teacher' means control freak. I haven't considered jobs or what I'll be when I grow up. I still need to get through school.

Maybe identity is how you behave. Mom lies, Dad goes along with Mom, and Brendan's trying to believe he's special. I don't want to be like _any_ of them. Is my face a mass of scars too? Is that what happens when you hide the truth? I'm not scared of scars you can see. But I'm worried about the hidden ones. Can honesty keep the scars away?

Linn

Walker

Gurke

Chapter 4
Bella's Day

MOST PEOPLE COMPLAIN ABOUT summer in California being too hot. But our swim team holds practices in the coldest lap pool in the state. "I may never get warm," I complain to my showerhead. Turning off the water, I step out, wrap myself in a robe, and twist a towel around my head. Moving into my room, I hang the towel on my closet door and shimmy into my favorite jeans, t-shirt, and sweater.

The mirror on my closet door silently waits for attention. I move closer and consider myself. "Crap. I forgot that pool chemicals dye my eyebrows." I pull the towel down and begin drying my hair. When I drop the towel and look back at the mirror, I let out a small squeak. "Brendan, what are you doing in my room?"

"Admiring me, myself, and I." He preens for the mirror. Then he focuses on my reflection. "You need a better shampoo, one that removes chlorine from your... eyebrows. That color is somewhere between boogers and puke."

"Thanks for the compliment," I grumble. "My shampoo does work on chlorine. I just forgot to... you know."

"What're you going to do about Mom's birthday?" Brendan gives his hair a finger comb and turns away from my mirror. He plops into my beanbag.

I pick up a brush from my desk and begin working out the knots in my hair. "Stop plopping. You're going to break my only purple-ish possession."

"I bought it. I own it." Brendan smirks.

"It was a gift. Doesn't that mean I own it?" I try to match the expression on his face.

"A gift isn't forever, Spaz. It's like a loan. You get to keep this in your room, but I gave it to you and can repo it if you fall short on your payments."

"What payments?"

"You know—being a good sister." Brendan pauses to think. "And anything else I consider necessary."

"So that means I can repo the sweats I bought you last year for Christmas?"

"Sure..." Brendan's voice betrays the trap I just walked into. "But you might want to wash them first. You don't even want to consider what bodily fluids are in those sweats."

I give Brendan the talk-to-the-hand salute and reach for my SPF lotion with the other hand. "Stop. You're disgusting. Why couldn't I have an older sister?"

"Just lucky, I guess." Brendan brushes off his shoulders. "But seriously, we've only got a few days until Mom's birthday. Any gift ideas?"

"I'm thinking of asking Dad for money," I say through closed eyes as I rub lotion on my face. "Then we could go to the shopping center."

"Are you a complete dimwit? No!" Brendan wags his finger at me. "There's no way I'm taking you shopping."

I put my lotion down and step back to my mirror. Studying my face, searching for scars...

Brendan's reflection in the mirror stares at me like I've lost it.

"Am I like Mom?"

"What the hell is wrong with you?" Brendan's demands.

"Well, it's genetic. Isn't it? We all end up like our

parents."

"Geez, Linn. Listen to yourself. Genetics? You are such a nerd. I'd say you're more like Dad or his father. PaPa doesn't talk much, but damn... the man can put you to sleep with scientific crapola." Brendan considers me for a moment. "Let's get back to a topic we can solve—birthday gifts."

I sit at my desk. "But when I see my reflection, I know I'm related to Mom and... you know the way she is."

"Don't you listen to anything I say? Genes are more complex than they tell you in school—AND you are not a simpleton. You can make choices. I choose to be awesome, keep my mouth shut, and hope... no, *believe* in my ability to NOT be Mom. I told you all this." Brendan's face is turning red. "If you act like Mom, I'll knock the shit out of you."

"You're right—pounding required if I go total-Bella." I smile at Brendan, hoping I can repair Fault-line Linn's shakeup. *Maybe I'll become an actress. I'm good at faking happy.*

Brendan's shoulders relax a little. "We made breakfast for Mother's Day and dinner for Father's Day. We can't cook again. So, what were you thinking?"

"I saw a commercial for a burn-proof oven mitt. You can touch anything in the oven without getting hurt."

"Mom doesn't like job presents." Brendan begins to mimic Mom's teacher voice. *"I'm not your cook, maid, or gardener. I'm a person and I matter."* He reverts to his voice. "So—nothing for the house, nothing for cooking, and nothing for the yard."

"Okay, then a personal gift." I shake my head in disgust. "I refuse to buy her underwear."

"Gross." Brendan laughs. "Mom wants gifts that show her in the best light. Gifts that help her believe she's perfect."

I stop myself before I ask if he means 'awesome.' *I*

could become an author and write a children's book—See Linn run. See Linn jump. See Linn shut it. "Dad always gets flowers, so we can't use that idea. Besides, she doesn't like flowers."

"I know." Brendan leans forward and reaches for my SPF lotion. "She acts like Dad's so thoughtful until he leaves. Then she goes off on men who stop on the way home to buy flowers. What's that about?"

"Guess she thinks he didn't remember until the last minute. I can see where she gets the idea. I saw a guy leaving the store with flowers on Mother's Day at five p.m. Dude—you couldn't have done this earlier in the day?"

"It's tough being a guy." Brendan squishes his eyebrows together. "We have to find the perfect gift to stay out of trouble."

"Oh, puh-lease. The gift should be about the recipient and not keeping yourself out of trouble." I point at Brendan's seat. "Take my beanbag for instance. You bought a lilac beanbag because you were thinking of me."

Brendan shakes his head. "No, Idjit. I bought this color because it was on sale. Geez, Linn, saving money's important."

"So, when you buy a gift, you're thinking of what serves *your* needs? Not sure I believe you." *There's an idea for what I can be when I grow up. I'll be a personal shopper for clueless guys like Brendan.*

Brendan stands, puts my lotion back, and stretches. "Tell you what—I'll buy Mom a gift that serves my needs and you come up with something personal. Let's see which gift she likes best."

I stand to face Brendan. He's not tall but I still have to look up. "Challenge accepted. But I still need a ride to the store. And stop using my lotion." *It's hard to act tough when you can't drive.*

"Sorry, Bubbles—the lotion is part of a good sister tax.

And, as far as driving to the store? You're on your own." Brendan walks out of my room laughing.

I grab my phone, fall onto my bed, and hit my Craft First app. I type in 'gift ideas' and scroll down to 'gift ideas for mom.' It's listed about six search titles down. People must search gift ideas for girlfriends and boyfriends more often than moms. *What does this say about me? It probably means I would be a terrible personal shopper.*

I grab 'Myrtle the pen' and a pad to copy down the cheap and easy category. *I know what this says about me— broke and lazy.*

* * *

"I'll get it," I yell and walk toward the front door.

Who am I talking to? Of course, I'll get it. I'm the only one in the room to hear the bell. Mom's in her bedroom, as usual. Dad's in the kitchen cleaning and shows no signs of stopping. Glancing through the side window, I see a woman with a pile of bright pink luggage. She's a brunette. About three inches shorter than I am. If you remove all the excess makeup, she would be—average. The muscle under my left eye begins to twitch. *A crazy multiplier is standing on the porch.*

"Aunt Lily's here," I shout while opening the door.

"Hey there, Sweetie. Help me with my bags."

I grab an oversized suitcase and drag it to the door. I almost drop it when I notice the paisley pattern—yuck. Three more matching bags sit on our porch. I slow down when Brendan enters the foyer, hoping for help.

Aunt Lily steps in front of Brendan. "Look how big you've gotten. Come here, Cupcake, and hug your Auntie."

Brendan complies while mouthing the words, "Help me" over her shoulder.

"Aunt Lily, we didn't expect you," Brendan says as he escapes her grasp.

"I was expecting her," Dad says as he emerges from the kitchen. "I invited Lily as a surprise for your mother's birthday." Dad gives her a side hug. "Bella will be thrilled."

I doubt the truth in those words. Aunt Lily's four years older and they've never been close. Another lie—Mom hates her. Besides, the house hasn't been cleaned. Mom usually makes us scrub everywhere when anyone is about to visit. *Dad seems oblivious to Mom's issues. Maybe I could train his eye muscles to twitch like mine.*

"She's in the bedroom. Come say hi." Dad directs Aunt Lily toward the back room.

"What's going on? Why is Aunt Lily here?" Brendan asks me once they're gone.

"Your guess is as good as mine. Help me drag this luggage inside."

"Where do you think she'll sleep?" Brendan grabs the smallest bag. "She should share a room with you. Both of you being girls, you know."

"My room's too small. Let's just leave these in the family room for now," I say, hoping Aunt Lily won't be staying in my room.

* * *

"What the fuck!" Brendan rushes into my room, slams the door, and drops into the beanbag.

"What's wrong? What happened?"

"Mom, Dad, still..." He shakes his head and drops it into his hands.

"Calm down. Tell me about Mom and Dad."

"Still doing it," Brendan mumbles.

"What are they doing?"

"The evil deed! Don't look at me like the moron you are. You know, knocking boots? Slamming cheeks? Geez, Linn, you are so clueless. Sex, our parents are having sex."

"Oh my God, did you see them?"

"No, yuck. Aunt Lily told me Mom's pregnant. I don't think she was supposed to tell but it slipped out."

"Mom can't be pregnant. She's turning thirty-nine. I mean, do her eggs even still work?"

"Aunt Lily says it's true. Ugh. Sex will never be the same for me."

"The same? Have you... no, don't tell me. I can't have those pictures in my head. It's bad enough that Mom and Dad... never mind." I leave Brendan moaning in my room and find Dad in the kitchen with his head in the fridge.

"Linn, acid or base?" Dad holds up a container of questionable foodstuffs.

"Maybe tomato sauce? Acid." *This is one of Dad's favorite games. Every time he cleans the kitchen, I have to identify the relative alkalinity of various items. Dad must want me to be a food inspector when I grow up.*

"Acid or base?" He holds up another container.

"Milk is a base but it's a trick question. I have to know what type of milk it is. Each has a different acidic level." I've had enough. "Is Mom going to have a baby?"

Silence.

Then, "Did Lily say something to you?"

"No, she told Brendan, and he told me. Is she?"

He straightens up and closes the fridge door. Face to face, no door between us. "Yes. Lily wasn't supposed to tell anyone, we wanted to share the news with you and Brendan ourselves. But since the beans have been spilled, we'll need you two to pitch in and help with Eric in November."

"Who? November?"

"It's a boy and his name will be Eric. Eric's going to change all our lives." Dad grins.

"All our lives? Brendan's going to college next year." My voice is too loud, and I try to tone myself down. "He's going to escape, the work and diapers. Aren't you too old for... babies?"

"Obviously not." Dad laughs. "That's why I invited Lily. She can help support your mother during the rest of her pregnancy."

"The rest of her pregnancy? Aunt Lily is staying here until November? That's months." My knees weaken with thoughts of the impending chaos. "Everything about this situation is wrong—and seriously disgusting."

Dad picks up the unwanted food jars and walks toward the garage, still laughing.

Why does he think this is funny? It's a total disaster. Aunt Lily staying here for months and now Mom is... I can't even think it. I pull my phone out and lock myself in the bathroom.

ME: OMG, Nadine, my mom is PREGS!!!!

NADINE: Haha, joking, right?

ME: NOT! Aunt L's here and says it's true... can you even??? Dad too - gross

NADINE: If she's having sex, yes.

ME: Ewwww don't say that - parents - ewwww-yuck-disgusto-noooo - going to wash out my ears, eyes, and brain - see you later and DON'T say that again

NADINE: Sorry, I'm here if you need me!

* * *

"Happy Birthday to Belladonna. Happy Birthday to you," Aunt Lily sings as she puts a plate of food in front of Mom. "And many more..."

"Don't call me that," Mom snarls.

"Why not? It's your name." Aunt Lily looks back and forth between Brendan and me. "Your Grandma Rose wanted to name your mother after an exotic flower. Unfortunately, the woman doesn't read much. Your mother's birth certificate actually says Belladonna, the name of a poisonous plant. We shortened it to Bella, a name so exotic it rivals my mashed potatoes."

Dad glances at Mom and interjects, "Thank you for remembering Bella's birthday, Lily."

"Oh, that's easy." Aunt Lily waves the comment away. "*Gone with the Wind* was published on June thirtieth. I remember because I'm so much like Scarlett."

"Published?" Brendan asks. "The movie *Gone with the Wind*?"

Brendan pulls his phone out of his pocket and holds it under the table. Technology isn't allowed at the dinner table. According to Dad, it slows down your digestive system. I'm sure Brendan's checking his multiple movie apps. Brendan's addicted to movies. He knows all sorts of useless information about films.

"We grew up in Wyoming, Lily—on a potato farm," Mom says. "We never went without food, and you don't have a southern accent. But there were always a lot of men around you. Like that farmer who used to show up with cow shit on his boots. What was his name?"

Brendan interrupts before Aunt Lily can respond. "The book was published in June, but the movie premiered in different places on days other than the thirtieth."

Aunt Lily raises a hand to her forehead and pretends to be faint. "I can't think about that right now. I have a birthday dinner to eat." She sits at our crowded dinner table and motions to our plates. "Enjoy."

Everyone's quiet while they consider how to eat this 'special' meal. Dad picks food off his plate and attempts to swallow. It shouldn't be a problem. Our plates contain baked chicken, corn on the cob, and Aunt Lily's not-so-exotic mashed potatoes. This is a typical meal in our house. However, Aunt Lily chose to plate the food and add spices for us. Now pepper covers the food, and I do mean 'covers.' Everything on the plate is the same color—gray-black chicken, gray-black mashed potatoes, gray-black corn. It looks like barf.

"Thanks, Lily," Mom breaks the silence, "but I don't feel well enough to eat. I guess morning sickness isn't limited to mornings."

"What about you, Sweetie?" Aunt Lily looks at me. "Don't you like chicken?"

"It's cooked well, but my science teacher says you shouldn't eat the skin. Too much fat." I move the over-peppered skin to one side of my plate.

"You brought a lot of luggage, Aunt Lily. How long are you staying?" Brendan asks.

I focus on eating the mashed potatoes from the bottom up, hoping to avoid the pepper on top. *Brendan isn't going to like this answer.*

"Not long, Cupcake. Long enough to take care of my baby sister. Bella the baby is having a baby." Aunt Lily laughs.

Mom's upper lip curls. The next thing she says is going to be a lie. When her lip curls, a lie is always next. *I could be a human lie detector if Mom was the only subject. Nope, that's a terrible idea.*

"We're so happy you're here, Lily," Mom mutters.

"Not long with all that luggage?" Brendan isn't paying attention to what's happening around the table. I attempt to catch his eyes but fail. "We have a washer and dryer."

"Oh no, Sweetie. The luggage is from the tour I took. It was perfection. A group of us went to South America. We saw all the best sights in Lima and then in Peru."

Dad stops eating and blurts out, "Lily, Lima's in Peru."

"George, you think I don't know where I've been. I got on the plane in Lima and I got off in Peru. I know these things." Aunt Lily gives a nod of finality.

Dad shakes his head and tries another bite of chicken. I covertly run my thumb across the corn and deposit the pepper flakes into my napkin.

Brendan pays me a semi-compliment. "Linn's good at geography. She could show you..."

Aunt Lily turns on Brendan with an attitude to rival any of Mom's drunken rants. "Don't make me look like a jackass, Cupcake."

This is why I don't want to become a travel agent—crazy people.

"Anyhow," Aunt Lily switches back to her fake sweet personality, "when George told me Bella was putting her old eggs to work, I decided to come here instead of going home."

"I'm going to bed." Mom grabs her tumbler of wine-type liquid and begins to stand.

"Bella, you can't leave before dessert." Aunt Lily nods toward Brendan. "My little man took me to the store, and we bought all the ingredients for a Piña Colada Birthday Bowl."

"Piña Colada?" Mom turns back to the table.

Aunt Lily knows how to get Mom's attention.

"And," Dad announces, "you have birthday gifts to open."

Mom's lip curls again. "I've gotten the flower arrangement you brought this morning."

Brendan raises his eyebrows.

"But there's more." Dad's not paying attention to Mom's lip curling. "I have another surprise for you. Expect delivery in July. I know it's late but it's still a birthday gift. Until then, I'm not talking."

"Ta-da." Aunt Lily deposits bowls in front of Mom and Dad. "My specialty for my aging sister. I'll get some Piña Colada bowls for us, kids."

I cringe. Aunt Lily can annoy Mom every time she speaks. Her words are bad enough, but the dessert—yuck. *The bowls look like a tropical drunk threw up. Pudding-coated chunks of what might be pineapple sit on top of crumbled yellow cake. The whole mess is covered with flaked coconut. I hate coconut.*

"Don't give me any, Aunt Lily," I shout into the kitchen. "I'm on a diet." *I need to become a chef if I want to survive my relatives.*

"Smart," Aunt Lily responds as she delivers a bowl for herself and one for Brendan.

I see why Mom dislikes her sister so much.

Brendan glances at me, then at his bowl, and back at me. He coughs once and I hear something that sounds like "itch." Mom and Dad taste the concoction carefully.

"I don't taste any rum," Mom says. "Doesn't a Piña Colada have rum in it?"

"It should." Aunt Lily laughs. "I left it out. You're pregnant. You can't drink."

Oh, snap! Brendan needs another 'itch' cough. I watch Mom to see what will happen next. She reaches for her tumbler while her face pinches together in every place possible. *Warning—contents under pressure will explode.*

"What's this?" We all look at Dad as he pulls a chunk of something out of his bowl.

"Oh, that." Aunt Lily reaches across the table and takes the lump with her napkin. "The bowl broke when I was serving up. I thought I got all the pieces but maybe not."

"The glass bowl?" Brendan asks as he pushes his dessert away.

"Yes," Aunt Lily responds. "I threw the rest of the recipe away just in case."

We stare at Aunt Lily for an extra-long moment. *Good thing I didn't want dessert. Disliking coconut is the smartest thing I've done today.*

Brendan breaks the silence. "Well... Linn and I have some birthday gifts to pass out." He reaches under the table and pulls out a package. "This is from me. Happy birthday."

Mom pushes her dessert out of the way and begins to unwrap Brendan's gift. Her lip curls again. "Thank you, Brendan. I've seen these oven gloves advertised." She turns to me.

I give Brendan a sideways glance as I reach under the table for my gift. "I made this myself." I pass a small box to Mom. "I know how much you like wildflowers. So I pressed these between books and turned them into a picture. There are two pieces of glass—I mean clear plastic—so you can hang it in the window like a sun catcher."

"Linn, what have you done?" Mom's voice is teetering on the edge of hysteria. "These are California poppies."

"Yes, I heard you say we have the prettiest state flower." My smile disappears as I watch my mother complete her Jekyll/Hyde transformation.

"It's illegal to pick poppies!" Mom points at me. "They could arrest you. And what will people say? They'll say you don't have responsible parents. Get rid of this where no one can see it." Mom begins to cry. "Nobody in this family loves me. Not even on my birthday."

"Bella," Dad says. "It was an honest mistake. We all love you."

I'm shocked into silence. *No, Linn. This isn't a surprise. Mom can never hear a truth she doesn't think up. She has to be perfect.*

Mom begins to rock back and forth, tapping her forehead rhythmically. "No, no, no. Nobody in this shitty family cares about me." She pops out of her chair, grabs her half-full tumbler, and storms out of the room.

I look at Dad. "I'm sorry. But it's not actually illegal."

"I'll check if everything's okay." Dad gets up and follows Mom out of the room without acknowledging my comment. *I guess he can't hear the truth either.*

"Guess I can't be a psychiatrist. I don't know how to help people."

"What are you talking about?" Brendan gives me a warning look as he tilts his head toward Aunt Lily. "Can we agree my present won?"

I get it. *Swallow your thoughts and act like everything's fine.* The words 'perfect' and 'perfection' bounce around in my head. "If you admit the oven glove was my idea. By the way, how does this serve your needs?"

"Mom will never use that glove. She'll put it in the grilling drawer, and I can use it outside." Brendan glances at Aunt Lily. "The weather will be good tomorrow. I'll grill something for dinner."

"Well, good." Aunt Lily beams. "That leaves us more time to gossip. Get my purse, Cupcake." Aunt Lily gives Brendan a brush-off wave. "I'll show you my pictures. Wait till you see the fantastic shots I took at Moocha-Poocha."

Shut it, I scream in my head. *Do NOT correct her pronunciation of Machu Picchu—breathe, breathe. Don't touch your eye, don't draw attention to your twitch.*

Brendan turns to Aunt Lily. "Where did you leave your purse?"

"In my room, of course."

"You mean Brendan's room?" I throw Brendan the best smile I can generate. "Oh, wait, his room is now the family room."

Brendan gives me the finger by pretending to scratch his nose.

* * *

Journal Entry – Summer Sale on Identities?

Brendan says I can decide my own identity and stop worrying about who I'm related to. Sorry genetics, I'm hanging onto this idea because I can't be related to these people—crazy, drunk, mean, lip-curling, lying psychos. I need to be okay, stable, and happy. The Fourth of July always has sales, and I need some new genes.

Dad should do something to stop her from drinking, right? He's a science guy. He knows Mom shouldn't drink. She should have stopped when she got... in... February. Oh crap, was it Valentine's Day? Yuck.

Brendan says the baby's a huge mistake and calls it 'Oops.'

Mom and Dad think I should not pick poppies—they think it's illegal. But I didn't do anything wrong and I don't want to throw Mom's gift away. Maybe one day I'll be brave and chase Mom around the house with it—poppy power!

LEAP
Finished the article on Personal and Emotional Development. It says I should have at least three good friends and belong to a group. I also need to feel safe. More expectations for my LEAP list...

7. ~~HAVE THREE GOOD FRIENDS, BELONG~~

Nadine's the only one I trust enough to be a good friend. I guess I'm doing what Brendan said and keeping my mouth shut. Will finding my identity help with LEAP 7? If I know who I am, will I have more friends? Or... if they get to know me and realize I'm a liar, will I have fewer friends? Going to call Alan and ask his opinion. Getting ready to be teased...

8. FEEL SAFE
Really? How am I supposed to feel safe? Mom's a pregger drunk. The only good thing is how much she hides in her room. Dad sides with Mom—search for 'denial' on the internet and there he is. Brendan's trying not to let his scars show. And Aunt Lily? She's cray-zee. How the H am I supposed to feel safe?

I used to read about local serial killers so I'd recognize the scary thing when it came for me. When I was ten, I realized the slasher movies are right—my biggest fear is in the house.

Need to consider my choices—run away from home and start over or stay here and start high school. Would it be easier to be a self-sufficient, honest person, and make new friends here or somewhere else?

Linn

Walker

Gurke

Chapter 5
Table Manners

I GOT ORIENTED LAST month for after school stuff and I've already started swimming. The learning side of school starts next month. Like really, really early in August. I'm not ready for learning, it's still too hot and now Aunt Lily's here and Mom's preggers! Life can't get worse. I thought summer was supposed to be for rest. If Mom doesn't stop waking me up so early, I'll probably get more sleep when I have to get up for school. Or when the baby comes.

Mom pulled some strings and got me enrolled in Honors English. It doesn't have anything to do with me. She needs to prove she's got smart children, even if it's not true. Now I have a reading assignment before school starts. Yeah, I'm ready for summer to be over but not for learning to begin, or continue, or whatever.

"Linn, we need you in the family room," Dad calls as he knocks on my door.

"Why? What's wrong?"

"Nothing's wrong. Why do you think something's wrong? Come talk."

"Because something is always wrong," I say to myself. I stick a tissue in the Ray Bradbury book and carry it out. Summer homework is the worse.

Mom and Dad are waiting in the family room.

"Can I get a drumroll?" Dad taps his fingers on the coffee table in a pantomime of drumming. "Bella's birthday present is being delivered today. I know it's a couple of weeks late, but now I can tell you. I bought a new kitchen table!"

"For my birthday?" Mom's upper lip begins to curl.

Obviously, Dad doesn't know about Mom's preferred gift list. Why is that? She's his wife.

"Yes," Dad says. "With the addition of Eric, the old one isn't large enough. There're four full-size people at dinner now and soon we'll be adding a highchair."

I try not to think about Brendan leaving for college next year.

Mom moves her facial muscles into what should be a smile. "That's... wonderful, George. What a great gift."

After considering her for a moment, I change the topic. "So, why do you need me?"

Dad drags his attention away from Mom's contorted expression. "Your mother and I have to go to the district preplanning meeting today. Brendan has taken Lily shopping. They'll deliver the table before anyone else gets home."

"So I should do—what exactly?"

"Open the door for the delivery guys. They'll take the old table and leave the new one. I paid for everything, except the tip. It's a heavy piece of furniture. Make sure they put the table in the right place and pay them for their effort." Dad hands me money from his wallet and turns to Mom. "You ready to go, Bella?"

Mom continues to stare into space for a second, shakes her head, and refocuses. I know how she feels. *It's difficult when your world shifts.* Mom's considering if a table is a good gift, *and I'm wondering why 'stranger danger' doesn't include delivery guys.*

"Have a good day," I say as they leave the house. "Hopefully I'll be alive when you return." I should add "unharmed" or "safe" but safe isn't an option in this house.

I sit down in my usual mealtime seat, pull out my phone, and send a new message to Nadine.

> ME: table being delivered - no one here but me - if I die, it was the delivery guys

> ME: gotta go - no need to respond - just saying

I sit back in my chair and run my hand over the table. *What do you say when a table leaves your life? Thanks for the memories?* I attempt to remember good times. I slide off my chair and sit on the floor under the table.

Yep, this is my strongest memory, Brendan and me on the floor under the table.

* * *

It was May and the school year was coming to a close. Being held back a year was tonight's dinnertime topic. I knew this wasn't about me or Brendan. I was excited about moving on to third grade so I wasn't paying attention.

Mom and Dad were arguing across their steaks about one of Mom's students, Rocky. This was not the first Rocky discussion.

Dad was talking physical development. "You've had Rocky in your classroom for two years now. He's getting to be a big boy. Time to move him forward, for the sake of the smaller children."

"What about Rocky?" Mom was channeling a caring personality. "He can learn if he stays with me."

"What do you think he can learn? He poured milk in the fish tank because he thought they looked thirsty." Dad shook his head. "He's six years old and didn't realize that fish would suffocate in milk."

Wait, my goldfish? "What? Are you talking about the fish I won at the school fair? The ones Mom told me to share with her class got suffocated in milk? All three of them?" I got no response.

"It was an honest mistake," Mom countered. "If I keep Rocky in kindergarten for one more year, I can teach him to read and he'll be ready for first grade."

Dad shook his head in frustration. "You haven't taught him to read in two years. What do you think you are, perfect?"

"So, are my fish all dead?" I interrupted. "Why didn't—"

Thwack!

Oh crap. Dad was sitting very still and looking down at the steak knife Mom had thrown. It was sticking out of his chest. Slowly Dad reached up to remove the knife. That's when I made eye contact with Brendan. With an unspoken agreement, we slid from our chairs to the floor. We sat with our knees pushed against each other, shaking. Brendan was small for a fifth-grader and the table wasn't large. I remember hoping it would protect us.

Brendan mouthed the words, "She's done it now."

"Can she throw a knife?" My voice squeaked in near hysteria.

"Normally she can't, uncoordinated."

Even then I knew when Brendan was trying to sound calm for me, but I couldn't force the fear out of my voice. "How do we get out of here?"

"Listen," Brendan hissed. "Do you hear anything?" We both inched up the table far enough to see over the top.

Dad had removed the knife and was pointing it at Mom. "Don't. Ever. Do. That. Again." Each word exited through his clenched teeth. There was a small spot of blood on Dad's shirt. The lack of bleeding made me feel better. But his quiet tone was frightening.

Mom started to cry. "I didn't mean to hit... I didn't think I could... I'm so sorry."

Dad stood and walked out of the room. Mom followed suggesting a hospital visit. Dad shook his head no. Brendan and I slid back under the table in case of more flying knives.

"Boy, he's pissed." Brendan breathed, "She's lucky to be alive."

"My fish are dead, suffocated with milk."

"Geez, Linn, you're an Idjit."

* * *

I sit quietly under the table as the Rocky memory fades. I look at my assigned Bradbury book. *Something Wicked This Way Comes*, no kidding. *Mr. Dark has nothing on my mom.*

I climb out from under the table when I hear the soft beeping of a truck backing up the driveway. I make it to the foyer and consider the delivery truck before opening the front door. The guy in the passenger seat exits and wipes his brow on his shirt. He walks to the back of the truck and waits for the driver to engage the brake. He lifts the cargo door, lowers the tailgate, and pulls out a purple clipboard.

Does he like purple? Anyone who likes purple must be trustworthy, right? I've never read about serial killers with purple clipboards. Besides, he doesn't look dangerous, only tired and thirsty. I could be a delivery person. I'm strong and I don't mind being sweaty.

"Hi, you need us to pick up and replace a table?" purple clipboard guy asks.

"Uh-huh," I respond. "Can I get you some water?"

"That would be fantastic, thanks."

I open the door wider. "Come on in."

The delivery guys break down the old table and push it to one side while I go get a couple of waters. It takes each guy three trips to bring in the chairs and table pieces. After about twenty minutes and more than three tools, the new table is up and ready. The guys take the waters and tip money. They thank me, stack the old chairs, and carry everything out in one trip.

As I lock the front door, I whisper my last goodbye. "Thanks for nothing, you lightweight piece of laminated trash. You will soon be forgotten, like Rocky and my goldfish."

I walk back into the dining area and check the new table. I run my hand over the tops of all six chairs and along the table's shiny, smooth oak surface. *Nice, solid chairs and a much larger eating area. I wonder how far Mom can throw a knife.* Sliding under the table I breathe in the smell of real wood. *This isn't a great birthday gift but it's a nice table. Brendan and I are both bigger now, but there's enough space under here for the two of us and one more. Just in case.*

I open my phone and check my previous messages.

NADINE: Serious? Are you okay?

ME: table here - nice - I survived -
all good sorry about the worry

I close my phone without waiting for another message.

I return to my room and retrieve my journal and Myrtle the pen. I lay down on the bed, close my eyes, and think about the escape list I started yesterday. *What comes first? Money, money, and money! No wonder Dad's so focused on how much things cost. I can't figure out how to get out of this house without money.*

"You asleep?" Brendan barges into my room and sits in my not-a-gift beanbag. He holds his head in his hands. "Never again. Never!"

I sit up and lean forward on my bed. "Never again, what?"

"Shopping with Aunt Lily." Brendan leans back and

stretches his legs out. "I spent four hours looking for an Oops gift." Brendan makes air quotes around his nickname for the baby. "After multiple stores and tons of bathrooms, she bought one thing for the little mistake."

"What did Aunt Lily and her *little man* buy?" I use as much sarcasm as possible.

Brendan frowns at me. "Not you too. I've had enough abuse for one day."

"Sorry, I couldn't help myself. What did she buy?"

"She bought a bunch of shit. There was makeup, perfume, and underwear. I can never un-see the things she waved in my face." Brendan leans forward and points a finger at me. "Don't repeat this—but she asked my opinion on which cut of underwear to buy. She said the high cut makes her legs seem longer and thongs keep her from having a panty line. I tried to tell her a panty line's a good thing for women her age."

I bite the inside of my mouth, so I don't laugh. "But what did she buy for the baby?"

"A onesie." Brendan moans.

I can't hold back the giggle. "That seems like a reasonable gift."

"You haven't seen it yet. It's a god-awful color of orange with lime green writing. It says, 'My aunt is the family hottie.'" Brendan shakes his head. "And she bought a matching green shirt for her that says, 'I'm the hottie.' I may never recover."

I wipe tears of laughter away from my eyes and take a deep breath to control my voice. "What can I do to help?" I ask as sincerely as I can before busting out again.

"Let me hide in your room until after Mom sees Aunt Lily's shirt. Her hottie-ness is going to cause a complete meltdown. Aunt Lily has taken over my bedroom and it's safe here," Brendan exhales.

I pick up Myrtle and my journal.

"What are you doing?" Brendan asks.

"Writing about the word 'safe.' This room could be our S.A.F.E. Zone. Sibling Avoidance of Family Errands."

"You *are* twisted, Spaz." Brendan attempts to complain, but his smirk suggests he enjoys making fun of me.

For the next thirty minutes we talk about errands we plan to avoid. We both freeze when the sound of the garage door opening interrupts our list.

I whisper, "Mom and Dad are home."

"Act normal. No. Act happy." Brendan sits up straight in my beanbag chair. "Hand me that book. I'll say I'm quizzing you."

I grab my copy of *Something Wicked* and pass it to Brendan. We both strike a studious pose when we hear the door from the garage open.

"Hi, Mom. Dad. How was your day?" Brendan calls cheerfully as they walk past my open door.

"I'm going to lie down," Mom answers without looking into my room.

Dad follows her into the house and stops at my door. "Linn, did you bring in the mail?"

"No, but I'll go get it as soon as I finish studying." I'm hoping for an encouraging response, but Dad continues into the family room.

Brendan gets out of the beanbag chair and creeps up to my door. He turns and puts a finger to his lips. I scoot off my bed and stand behind him.

Mom's voice is clear. "Shit."

"What's wrong?" Dad asks.

"This damn table. Linn put it in the wrong place. You need to do something about her. She never gets anything right."

"The table's in the right place," Dad says. "It's just larger than the old one."

Did Dad just defend me? I relax a fraction until I hear

Mom again. "What the hell's that?"

"This ol' thing?" Aunt Lily responds. "It's a t-shirt I bought today. Don't you like it?"

"You need to exchange that for a larger size." Mom's voice sounds sweet—a shiver travels up my spine. *Aunt Lily should run.* "The seams will split and that's a terrible color. You should get the shirt in dark brown. I read somewhere that brown's a slimming color."

Brendan and I exchange a wide-eyed glance. *Uh-oh.*

I expect to hear anger from Aunt Lily but her voice is calm. "Oh no, Sweetie, this color matches the cute little onesie that I found. See?"

I imagine Aunt Lily holding up an orange/green baby shirt. If Mom were a fly, Aunt Lily would pull off her wings and enjoy watching her struggle.

"What are you doing?" Mom shouts suddenly. "This isn't about you. It's *my* family and *my* baby."

"Well," Aunt Lily responds. "You're right about one thing. I'm not a pregnant cow."

"What you are..." Mom stammers. "What you are is pathetic. You're jealous because I'm prettier and I have a husband who stays with me."

"Bella," Dad interjects using his calming voice meant to keep Mom from flying off the handle. "I don't think you need to—"

Mom isn't listening to Dad. "You tell people you're younger than me but you're not fooling anyone. You are aging—poorly! The makeup isn't hiding the wrinkles, and your roots are showing a lot of gray."

"Have you been drinking, again?" Aunt Lily asks. "Being an alcoholic at home's bad enough. Do you drink at work too? Your coworkers must smell the booze on your breath."

Brendan and I lean away from the door. I cover my mouth to keep quiet. Brendan's head begins to swivel around but snaps back when we hear the slap.

Pop!

For a minute there's silence, then Dad's teacher voice demands attention. "Bella, Lily. Stop this, both of you."

"You bitch!" Aunt Lily's shaky voice cuts Dad off. "Nobody loves you because you don't deserve to be loved."

Wow, those words sound familiar, but they're coming from Aunt Lily, not Mom. These two are both messed up. Maybe having a brother is better than having a sister.

"Get out!" Mom screams. "Get out of my house!"

Now the only sound is feet stomping down hallways. *Aunt Lily will be leaving soon.*

Brendan turns around and whispers, "I hate when I'm right."

"Our S-A-F-E Zone's not only for avoiding errands." I pick up my journal again. "Now it's also for Staying Away From Erratic Events."

Brendan tilts his head sideways. "I don't understand how your brain works. The word 'Erratic' isn't strong enough to describe what happened."

"I know, but it's the only word for crazy that starts with an E."

* * *

Journal Entry – Joyless July

The reading assignment for Honors English isn't difficult. We're expected to explain a quote about how people who seem happy are full of sin. Duh... I can tell you all about joyless smiles. This book should be titled <u>Bella and Lily the Wicked, Are Here</u>. I'll get an A in this class— finally a good reason to live with my mother.

LEAP - MAYBE

I still don't know what or who I'll grow up to be. I want to keep working on my LEAP list but there's no progress.

LEAP 6, Know your identity.

My fish weren't the only pets that disappeared into Mom's Kindergarten Kill Room. Later, Mom took my hamster to <u>show</u> the kids in her room. Supposedly Goldie ran away—not sure I believe <u>that</u> excuse. Then two bunnies I hadn't owned long enough to name disappeared.

Pets are supposed to teach you to care. It didn't work—every time I love something, Mom takes it away. She said I needed to share with children who have less than me. I shared and they killed.

Brendan never owned any pets. Guess you can't kill what your child doesn't have. Mom and Aunt Lily suck all of the sanity out of our house. How can two people make a bigger mess than the rest of us are able to clean up?

After talking to Brendan, I know I need to wait until he goes to college to consider running away. Brendan needs me. Okay, he said he feels safe in my room, but I'm sure he means that he feels better with me around. Is Brendan a friend? Could I count him with Nadine? For LEAP 7, Have three good friends, belong. I need to think about this. Most of the time he's on my side.

Brendan's also worried about 8, Feel safe. What will it be like when Brendan leaves? Who will be safe with me? Maybe I could follow him to wherever his college will be.

Linn

Walker

Gurke

Chapter 6
Equal Wrongs

AM I PSYCHIC? I know what's coming and I want to get out of this car. As soon as we stop.

"Today's the first day in September. Do you know what that means?" Brendan pulls the car into his parking space at the high school.

"I knew you were going to say the same thing you said last week," I groan.

"This is the second month of me driving you to school. You owe me for all these rides."

"I know and I appreciate it." I try to sound thankful. "We only had a few weeks of school in August. Technically, that's not even one month."

Brendan gets out of the car. "Let's go, keep your head down and your mouth shut. When we leave this parking lot, I don't know you."

I exit the car and spread my arms. "Invisibility achieved."

I turn to see Brendan walking away. The word 'Idjit' floats back to me.

* * *

Another day defined by the fifty-minute shuffle.

Come on, everybody... sit, sit, sit, nod to the teacher, pretend to learn, sit, sit, sit. Now stand up and walk. Step to the right, step to the left, and squeeze through the bodies. Move quickly! And... stop. Grab the closest chair when you hear the bell.

Thankfully fourth period is P.E. and then lunch. Nadine's waiting for me outside the locker room.

"Hey, Linn. Big news... I have a date for the dance this month, Jimmy! You don't know him. He's in my math class. He's redoing math 'cause he failed the first time so he's older and can drive. How about you? I heard Steve Miller is going to ask you." Nadine laughs. "Has he asked yet? Do you two want to go with Jimmy and me?"

My mouth drops open. *What is she talking about? I've seen the posters about buying tickets, but I didn't think I'd be going to the dance and now this? Steve asking me to go? And Nadine knows about it before I do? Crap. I don't need this. Not today, not with Mom being preggers. Crap, crap, crap.* "No," I respond. "He hasn't asked and I hope he doesn't. 'Cause he's a hyperactive dweeb."

Nadine falls into a synchronized walk next to me. Mrs. Portia makes us take a towel as we enter the locker room. Like we're going to take a shower. *Not happening, Mrs. P, I'm not getting undressed in front of these bimbos. I haven't even undressed in front of my not-so-magic mirror.*

"Linn, are you okay?" Nadine's eyes show concern, but she isn't going to make me talk if I don't want to. She's that kind of friend.

I think about how angry I am with Steve, Nadine, Brendan, and of course, Mom. Then I lie again. "Just tired, I guess. Everything's fine. Steve has been around since they moved into the area in sixth grade. He's not a bad guy, I just don't want to date him!"

I walk up to the mirror in the changing room. "Do I have scars?" I know they are there. I can feel them getting deeper every time Mom drinks too much. But can others see them?

Nadine stands behind me and looks at me in the mirror. "What are you talking about? I thought we were still on the topic of Steve and the dance."

"Nothing, never mind. Life sucks. Let's go kick some balls," I joke. "Soccer balls that is." We leave the locker room laughing our 'let's not get too serious' laugh.

Mrs. Portia assigned teams at the beginning of the semester. She has a list created to mix ages and sexes into teams of equal abilities. We play a round-robin series of short, five-on-five games. I was happy when Mrs. P put Nadine and me on the same team. But I was thrilled when Javy was put on a different team. I figure the best way to impress Javy is to play well against him. Everyone loses to Javy. I plan to shut him down and win.

* * *

I run around the soccer field, celebrating. It's only early September but this counts as part of my birthday month. September's the best. It took three weeks of round-robin soccer, but we won. I shut down Javy! I know it's a team effort, but today I blocked three of his shots and stole the ball from him. Being left-handed also makes me left-footed, and it's difficult to get the ball once I have it under control. I can't shout it out loud but—*eat it Golden Boy!* All of my anger is channeled into winning. I didn't know I was going to pull a Brandi Chastain, but suddenly my shirt is in my hands and I'm thinking of sliding on my knees toward Javy. At the last minute I realize the knee slide takes skill and I'd probably end up bloody and unable to walk. I stop running without knowing what to do. *Smooth, Linn. Real smooth!*

"Linn Gurke!" Mrs. Portia's voice could break glass. "Put that back on... this instant."

"What? I have on a sports bra. And Brandi Chastain did it." I glance around. Everyone has frozen.

Except for Nadine, who's bent over, trying not to laugh. "The girls are out," she blurts.

All the other students are standing still and gaping at me. Even Javy. I've succeeded in shocking almost everyone and now he knows I'm alive. *Crazy, but alive.* I slide my shirt back on as Mrs. P strides up to me. She has 'the finger of truth' out and pointing to the stadium exit.

"Principal's office, Gurke. Don't bother to collect your things, just go."

I leave the field while Mrs. P attempts to control the class. *Pretty sure I'm going to get grounded for this one* That should solve my dance problem. No shirt = no freedom = no dance = no Steve! I'm chicken and I know it. Getting grounded will keep Steve in the friend zone and I don't have to hurt his feelings.

My trip to the administration office is quiet. I study the empty courtyard and green space. At least it's not raining and I'm able to smell the eucalyptus. Maybe I could just sit on the grass and breathe. No, Mom and Dad would kill me if I skip out. Let's admit it, I'm toast. This is what I wanted, right? Punished, not dead. Suck it up, Linn. You are alone, as usual.

I avoid the covered walkways that connect a series of separate buildings. *I'm a rebel.* I don't need to use the footpaths. I can walk on the grass. Okay, it's actually dirt. Hard-packed, dried-out dirt.

Don't ask me why the school was designed as separate buildings. Since it's California, my guess is they were hoping to cut their losses during an earthquake or wildfire. Oops, there goes the sophomore wing and all the inhabitants! Good thing the junior wing is still intact. Did we lose the kid on her way to the administrative void? Doesn't matter, she wasn't important enough to be noticed.

Arriving at Principal Greene's office, I'm directed to one of the hard chairs outside his door. I know the wait is deliberate. I'm supposed to be 'thinking about your behavior, young lady.' Both of my parents are teacher types, so I've heard all about schools, and how they attempt to control children. I'm supposed to treat adults as equals, but teachers don't treat students as equals. Shouldn't adults behave better than us? They could start by not trying to control us, not assuming we're all bad. Besides, you think you can punish me? I know the laws that constrain teachers. They've got nothing that can hurt me. I save all my pain for home.

I spend my time contemplating logistics. *If I go to the locker room for my clothes, I'll miss lunch. Or, I wear my gym clothes for the rest of the day and get lunch.* Setting food as a priority seems reasonable. My stomach rumbles in agreement.

Mr. Greene opens his door and invites me in. He sits behind his desk in one of those roller chairs. Mr. Greene's a small, round man with a huge mustache. When he sits behind his desk, he looks like what you'd get if you mashed together a movie villain and a biker dude. *I doubt those short legs could straddle anything larger than my Schwinn.* I consider the office. Lots of pictures of Greene with politicians but no chair near enough for a conversation. I stand.

"Well, young lady. I believe this is the first time you have been to my office. Not a good sign." Mr. Greene seems to be enjoying himself. "What did you do to deserve this honor?"

"Our team won the soccer series in P.E." I attempt to focus on the positive.

"That's very special for your team. What'd you do?"

"I celebrated. I took off my t-shirt."

"You did what?" Mr. Greene's expression is no longer happy.

Well, I can match your unhappy. I'm angry at everyone and that includes you, Mr. Green. I think of Ms. Hess saying to 'show, not tell' in my writing, so I take my shirt off, again.

"I did this." *I am nothing if not a truth-telling, bad-girl rebel.*

Mr. Greene throws his hands in front of his face and leans away from me. The roller chair nearly tips him backward. He needs a lower center of gravity. Maybe if he'd shave off the overgrown snot mop?

Greene recovers just short of tipping over and sputters, "Put that back on. You can't... I can't... I know your father. He's an administrator in the next district. What would I tell him?"

By the time Mr. Greene peaks through his fingers, I have my shirt back on. "I have on a sports bra. You can't see anything." *I wouldn't show and tell with you even if I was a slut—which I'm not. At least I'm going to be grounded and don't have to go to the dance.*

"This is unacceptable. You're not allowed to take your shirt off at school."

"Javy Ramos takes his shirt off at the end of every soccer game. I did the same thing."

"Javy's a boy and it's different. Javy doesn't have... I mean, you're a girl and... Never mind. I'm not doing this, go see Ms. Garcia."

Wow, he sounds like Mom... I'm not doing this? Mr. Greene and Mrs. Portia have both pointed out the exit for me. Maybe I should keep going and leave the school. No, I can't be that rebellious. I walk down the hallway to the Vice Principal's office.

There's no wait at Ms. Garcia's door. I'm invited in when I knock on the door jam. Ms. Garcia stands, shakes my hand, and offers me a seat. Ms. Garcia's taller than I am but not by much. Her hair's a mass of soft, barely controlled curls. *I wish I had curls. Timesaving natural, free, curly hair I could wash, fluff, and go. I wouldn't have to braid my hair to give it body...*

I snap back to reality. There aren't politician pictures

in this office. A couple of diplomas and a watercolor of the Monterey Coast are the only decorations. The lighting and furniture arrangement gives the room a feeling of calm. Quiet and control in the same space. Ms. Garcia smiles and asks me to repeat my story—soccer, series, winning, shirt off, sent here.

Ms. Garcia responds using the same words, "You did what?"

By now I'm getting used to the routine and enjoying the shock value. So, I stand and remove my t-shirt. "I have a sports bra on. I'm not flashing anyone." *I'm such a rebel. Maybe my identity is more rebel than truth-teller. Either way, clarity's still a thing.*

Ms. Garcia tilts her head to look at me. "Nice bra. What color's that?"

"Lilac with blush accents. I like purple." My voice sounds lame, not rebellious.

"Very pretty. What brand?" Ms. Garcia doesn't seem shocked.

"Comfort Champ," I reply. "I got it on sale at the shopping center."

"I'll have to check it out." Garcia grins at me "Now, put your shirt back on. I can see you spent a lot of time on your hair today. Waterfall braids, right? All this dressing and undressing is undoing your work. Tell me again, why did you take your shirt off?"

"We won the soccer series. Against Javy Ramos. I was celebrating. I just did the same thing Javy does every game, win or lose. It's not fair, girls have to keep our shirts on while guys can go around half-naked all the time."

"And why do you think Javy takes his shirt off?" Ms. Garcia's voice tells me she already knows what my answer should be.

"He likes to show off his abs?"

"And those games are held during extra-curricular

activities. We try not to regulate student behavior after school hours. We don't condone Javy's behavior, but we leave it to the coach to manage his team. Besides, Javy may not realize it, but his antics are a joke. People don't take him seriously. Tell me, why did you take off your shirt today? Was it really about equality?"

Ms. Garcia's talking to me like an adult. I decide to try a little honesty.

"No. I wanted attention. Still, it's not fair and it makes me angry."

"I understand completely. I know how frustrating the double standards are for girls. But, equality isn't about acting like men. That isn't an appropriate answer for anyone. Let alone a grown woman."

Garcia says I'm a woman. My eyes begin to sting.

"We don't need to lower ourselves to simple attention-seeking. We behave with strength, pride, and nobility because we embody all of those traits. You embody all of those traits, Linn."

I sniff and rub my nose. I tell myself not to cry.

Ms. Garcia's brows furrow and her face sags into regret. She continues, "Unfortunately you misbehaved during school hours, and I do have to be fair. You will be going to detention and expected to keep your shirt on for the rest of this year. If possible, stay clothed for the rest of high school. Still, I'm going to let you pick the day you'll attend our after-school confinement. We can schedule your punishment when your brother's staying late. That way I don't have to call your parents about today's clothing decisions. I'll leave it up to you to discuss the situation with the appropriate people." Ms. Garcia looks at me for a moment. "Linn, if you need to talk to anyone, I'm here. I know you're angry about the world being unfair, but if there's more..." Another pause stretches out between us. "Maybe later? Now you better get back on schedule."

Maybe I'm not a truth-teller. I'm not sorry about the shirt thing. But, people don't often express faith in my behavior. It's confusing.

I blink my eyes too many times and swallow the lump in my throat. I force my feet to move toward the door. There are no pointing fingers, just high expectations.

This is a new type of hurt. Don't cry, don't cry. Why do I want to behave for Ms. Garcia? Why don't I tell her to go stuff herself because I'm a rebel who wants to be punished? Why didn't I say something about Mom's drinking? Chicken!

* * *

At the end of the day, I'm still wearing my gym shorts. I go back to the locker room for my clothes and head for Brendan's parking place. There aren't many benefits to having an older brother at the same school, even when he gives me a ride home. Today the ride comes at a cost. Javy and Brendan are deep in conversation by the trunk of his car. There must be a game tonight because Javy's wearing his gold soccer uniform. I know Javy's ratting me out to Brendan, but the gold material complements Javy's skin in a way that melts my irritation. All I can do is look dumb and say, "Hi guys."

I plop into the passenger seat of the car and wait for Brendan to join me. *What happened to Linn the rebel? Will Linn the truth-teller speak up? If so, get out of the car and tell Javy how you feel. Maybe tomorrow.* I watch the side view mirror as Javy turns away from the car. People in the mirror are more clueless than they appear. Javy heads back to the fieldhouse for his game. Even tomorrow might be too soon for truth-telling.

Brendan slides behind the wheel and slams the door. He pulls out of the parking lot before he speaks. "What did you do?"

"Come on, Brendan. I know Javy snitched. I shouldn't

have to repeat this, but I'll say it slowly for you. I... took... my... shirt... off."

"Geez, Linn, what were you thinking?"

"My team won the entire soccer series, against Mr. Gods-Gift-to-Gold-Uniforms. Besides, Javy takes his shirt off all the time."

"Yeah, well Javy's fit. He has a six-pack. And you..." Brendan gives me a quick once over, "have boobs."

"Technically, Javy and I both have the same thing. They're mammary glands."

"No, those are absolutely not the same thing. What am I supposed to say when we get home? I'm not telling Mom and Dad. That's your job."

I slouch into the front seat and close my eyes. "Thanks for nothing, Bro."

Brendan and I are silent the rest of the way home. *For us, silence is not the same as quiet. If body language can be heard, we're both shouting.*

Mom always tells me to just get it over with, like ripping a Band-aid off quickly. "Mom?" I shout as we enter the house. "I flashed the goods at school."

Mom doesn't usually get home before we do, but lately, she's been early. Today she still has her work clothes on and turns to us with a hopeful look. "What goods? Was something good?"

"The goods." Brendan throws his arms up in response to her confusion. "You know, the bouncing Buddhas? Humpty and Dumpty? Geez, Mom, she showed her tits."

Mom's skin goes ashen.

"Brendan's exaggerating. I only took my shirt off when we won our soccer series, the whole series. I had my sports bra on. Come on, Mom. The girls were covered and controlled." I give Brendan an accusatory glare as if he's the one misbehaving.

"Stop it, both of you," Mom squawks. "Linn, your

birthday is canceled. If you're going to be a slut at school, we won't spend money on you or celebrate you. This discussion's done."

"I'm not a slut. This had nothing to do with sex. It was about winning at soccer. I have to go to detention. Ms. Garcia said so. Are you going to ground me?"

"Ms. Garcia knows you're a slut? Linn, your father and I have to see her at the cross-district meetings. How could you do this to us?" Mom's voice cracks with tears and she taps her head before pointing at me. "No. Deal with this and don't mention it again. No birthday for you."

"Mom, Ms. Garcia doesn't think I'm bad. She said I'm better than—"

"No. This topic doesn't exist. You hear me? I say it didn't happen and it didn't." Mom grabs her tumbler and heads for the liquor cabinet.

"Geez Linn," Brendan whispers. "You need to keep your shirt on."

* * *

The next week, Brendan has a Student Government meeting after school. I head to detention secure in the knowledge I don't have to ask Mom for a ride home. Dad's still unaware of my fashion or lack of fashion choices. By the time he got home the other night, Mom was well on her way to Defcon One and even Brendan knew to be quiet.

Detention's one of those rotating teacher responsibilities. Today's keeper of depraved children is Ms. Hess. She's in her sixth year of teaching but seems older. Short stature, solid build, and a blondish chin-length bob. Despite her height, Ms. Hess controls her classroom. She's my favorite teacher but I've avoided her since last week when I wrote a story about living with alcoholism. I look around the room for someone who might keep Ms. Hess busy so I can fly under the radar. I'm hoping for one of the hyper-kids who attempt to escape every classroom. Unfortunately, detention is short on hyper desperados today. There are two guys I don't know sleeping on their desks, and Alan. *Oh crap, now I have to tell Alan what I did. Honesty is a full-time job. I can't pick and choose when I am a truth-teller. Suck it up.*

Alan waves me over to a seat next to him. As usual, he has his sketchpad out and is working on his next craft fair project. "What ya in for?" Alan whispers.

"Lewd and lascivious behavior," I respond.

Alan snorts.

"What about you? What did you do?" I know it's easy to distract Alan by getting him to talk about himself.

"I was late, but only a little. I missed half of first period. Honestly, this is so absurd. As an officer in the Key Club, I was helping count the election results. By the way, congrats to Brendan for his big Senior Class Rep win. Big B's got a three-year winning streak."

"Big B? I don't think I've ever heard anyone call Brendan that."

"Anyhoo, I stayed at school until dark. You'd think they'd give me a break the next day and let me show up a little late. But nooo. Detention slap and thanks for nothing, dude. Sucks that doing something good got me sent here. Now I know how my ancestors felt. So unfair."

"Your ancestors?"

"Girl, you have got to pay attention to our state history. The Spanish took my ancestors' homes and made them build a mission on their own land. Our history's full of Native Americans used as free labor and then punished. Like me."

I try to act sympathetic after Alan's comparison of his detention to real suffering by his ancestors, but I lose it and let out my own snort, followed by a giggle attack.

Alan stares at me until I control the giggles. "Who says

girls are understanding?" he complains and gives me the talk-to-the-hand salute.

"Ms. Gurke, please join me at the front of the room." *Oh crap. Ms. Hess doesn't sound like she's making a request.*

I swallow my giggles and drag my feet as I walk to the front of the class. There's a chair next to the desk. It's strategically turned so any occupant will have their back to the rest of the room. *I imagine my father describing seating designs. Teacher-student conversations remain private, and no one leaves the room.*

Sitting down in the chair, I bow my head and avoid eye-contract. "Ms. Hess?"

"Linn, I've been trying to talk to you about your English essay. Is everything okay at home?"

"Yes, ma'am, everything's fine." *Liar, liar, denial on fire.*

Ms. Hess scoots her chair toward me and lowers her voice. "I know what it's like to live with alcoholism, Linn. My father was larger than life and everyone's favorite party guest. But when he got home it was a different matter. He was like Mr. Dark in our Ray Bradbury book, he reveled in the fear he caused his children. My brother and I had to find ways to survive."

I force myself to sit up in the chair and give Ms. Hess a practiced smile. "It was only a story. Everything's good." I feel like crap as the lies dribble over my lips. I just blew my LEAP 6 identity out of the water. Speaking up and being honest didn't last long. I'm not a truth-teller, not a rebel. I'm my mother—no, I'm not a drunk evil witch. I'm my father—in denial. I'm my brother—keeping secrets. I'm my family values—shutting the fuck up.

"When children take their shirts off at school, they might be expressing anger."

"You know about that?" I squeak.

Ms. Hess laughs softly. "It was the talk of the faculty room. I have to say, don't quote me on this, I was proud of you. Showed some gumption. Still, I'm worried about you. What's happening to cause you to misbehave?"

I shake my head slowly and continue to avoid eye contact. "I appreciate your concern, Ms. Hess. But my life's pretty good compared to others." *Why am I excusing Mom's behavior?*

"That's what we all say. I know what you're thinking, Linn. I've been in your shoes. You believe 'If I pretend everything's fine, it will be true.' Right?" Ms. Hess waits for an answer.

"That's what Brendan said," I mumble.

"Yes." Ms. Hess chuckles. "Brendan's a great example. Did you know there're studies to support Brendan's attempts to bend reality? One study concluded that if you force yourself to smile when you are sad, your body begins to produce dopamine. Dopamine helps improve your attitude. It's a very useful tool. But you have to be careful, Linn. There's a fine line between using mind over matter and denial. Do you understand?"

Ms. Hess dips her head and forces me to look at her. "Smiling to improve your attitude can't hurt you. But denial is dangerous. You aren't simply bending reality; you are saying it doesn't exist. Be careful Linn, don't let lies become your truth."

I plaster a smile on my face. *Why can't this woman be my mother? Why can't I have a mother who cares about being honest? Or one who likes me more than her bottles. Ms. Hess said smiling doesn't hurt you. Don't cry, don't cry. Get through today without crying.*

Ms. Hess sighs. "I want you to know you can talk to me about anything. Unless you describe illegal behavior, I won't repeat what you say. Teachers must report physical abuse and unlawful acts. Just so you know."

"Thank you, Ms. Hess. I'm sorry I misbehaved and ended up in detention."

"Don't worry Linn. Just between us, I think people who don't get sent to detention at least once during high school are boring." Ms. Hess's smile nearly releases my tears.

I walk back to my seat.

Alan gives me a sideways glance. "What'd she say?"

"Nothing I can repeat. I'm not allowed to talk about my life. I absolutely hate it. Ms. Hess is the worst." *I keep my head down and hope the tears will evaporate.*

"I don't think she's bad. But if you say so, I'll hate her too. What do we hate the most about her? Tell me and I'll spread it around school."

"Hess and Garcia... both... so detestably... nice."

"Garcia?" Alan looks confused. When I don't respond he says, "Whatever," gives me a 'she's crazy' eye-roll, and goes back to his sketch.

I pick up my backpack, move to the row of chairs that have computers and open up an internet search. Looking up what the CDC says about pregnancy and alcohol gives me more information than I need. Apparently, there are spectrums and syndromes caused by drinking. And every woman has to worry about postpartum. Remind me never to get pregnant. Or have sex for that matter!

All the pictures make me feel dizzy. I decide homework is a better solution. Ms. Hess is watching me, but math isn't getting through to my brain. I slowly slide my phone out of my backpack and place it between my textbook and notepad. While pretending to do homework, I open up Snapchat.

NADINE: When can we go shopping? Dance!!

ME: Depends on if I get grounded, so far nothing

NADINE: Anything for my BFF - let me know

ME: detention - talk later

NADINE: Seriously, ANYTHING

I stare at my math book thinking of the message I'd like to send to Mom. *Be warned, Mom. I'm dealing with this and not talking. But the spiteful part of me is difficult to control.*

* * *

Journal Entry – Virgo the Ageless

I took my shirt off at school. Why is that a bad thing? I had to go to detention, so what. If I listen to Ms. Hess, detention might belong on the good list. But I don't feel good about it, mostly because I lied to her. I wanted to be punished but I don't think detention's a punishment. Disappointing good people is much worse.

I told Dad about taking my shirt off. I had to tell him if I wanted to be grounded before the school dance. Both Mom and Dad are angry. Still haven't been grounded. How am I going to avoid hurting Steve's feelings when he asks me to the dance? I have to ask someone else... but not Javy.

My birthday's been canceled—my fourteenth birthday! I never thought it would be a big deal. But I'll still be a year older, right? If you cancel your birthday, does it cancel the whole year?

Virgos are too practical to hit anyone. Considering bitch-slapping my mom. Might change my zodiac sign to a chicken.

LEAP - REVIEW
I don't think I'm making enough progress on my list.

Linn's Emerging Adult Plan (LEAP)

Parts 1 & 2

Growth spurt ✓

Body development ✓✓

Start period   Still nothing! I know there's something wrong with me!

Be self-sufficient   Too young to drive. Haven't made any money since the garage sale!

DATING AND PREFERENCE
I beat Golden Boy at his own game. That's not going to help with dating but at least he noticed me. Well, he noticed my sports bra. I have no chance with this guy. And what would I do with him if I did get the chance?

FIND YOUR IDENTITY
I don't think honesty is part of my identity. Am I lost because I wasn't a truth-teller? I

haven't found any scars on my face, but I feel them burning red inside me. I'm worried my internal scars will mark me forever. Is that what's happening to Brendan?

HAVE THREE GOOD FRIENDS, BELONG
Seems I'm going backward on this one. Nadine's still my friend and Alan talks to me but I think he's only interested in Brendan. If I don't come up with a dance alternative soon, I'll lose Steve as a friend.

FEEL SAFE
That's a laugh, not!

In summary—It's only September and this year can't get any worse. I have no control over my physical development (LEAP 1, 2, and 3), I can't drive, I'll never date, and I don't know who I am (LEAP 4-8 seem hopeless). I told the truth, then I lied, then I was a rebel, then I felt guilty about detention, then I told the truth again and I don't know if I should feel bad because Dad's disappointed. Should I care about Mom being angry? Sorry, I don't care. She can kiss my not-getting-older booty.

Linn

Walker

Gurke

Chapter 7
Ignite the Nite

My birthday's tomorrow and it's still canceled. Mom didn't ground me, so I used Alan to solve my dance problem. Last night I opened Snapchat to double-check.

> ME: good dance lessons the
> other day - you still okay going
> with me?

> ME: as friends?

> ALAN: yes, as friends!

> ME: thanks

> ALAN: Not needed - our
> deal - U joined K Club

> ME: and signed up for a fundraiser!!!

> ALAN: Abso-lut

Canceling my birthday means no presents, no cake, and no special birthday things. Pretty sure Mom won't un-cancel anything that means more work for her.

I turn when Nadine speaks. "What do you think I should do with my hair, Linn?" Nadine's sitting on my bed, painting her nails a deep jade. "I saw a video on Bantu knots but I don't think my hair's long enough."

I drag my brain back to the here and now. "I liked the style you did last Saturday. What did you call it? A twist-out? I love the natural look on you." I'm not good with nail polish so I'm using my desk to steady my hands as I struggle to smooth out the lavender.

"What about your hair?" Nadine's inspecting the finished paint on her hand.

Nadine's a great friend. She listens and cares. I haven't been completely honest with Nadine but she's still there for me. "I'm sticking with waterfall braids. It shows off the highlights in my hair." I grab the nail polish remover for the lumps I've created. "Why so much trouble for Jimmy? I thought you weren't into him."

"The trouble is for me, not him. But Jimmy is a good date. He's old enough to drive. Still, not as pretty as Alan the Gorgeous Jeweler."

"Alan's a friend. We're going as friends." *Can I count Alan as friend number two? He listens, sometimes. I trust him. Not like a boyfriend. But as a boy who's a friend.*

"Why? Didn't anyone else ask? I heard that—"

"Stop right there." I hold up my only successfully polished finger. "Steve asked but Alan and I'd already made plans. Besides, I'm not interested in Steve." I'm struggling with a second nail. "I still think Jimmy's too old for you. But we're riding together, right?"

Nadine blows on her nails to help them dry. "I'm not tied down. If you're only Alan's *friend* I might check him out." Nadine reaches for the glitter topcoat from her nail art kit.

"Do what you want. But, Alan's not going to be anything more than a friend, take my word for it." *I don't want to say too much. This is Alan's story. He's the one who should tell it. I can't say too much because I care about both Nadine and Alan. Good friends are a lot of work. Maybe that's why you only need three. It would be too much to keep up with more than three.*

"Why can't we turn this into a birthday party?"

I keep my head down. "Mom's father preached that girls become evil when they grow into women. I don't want to remind Mom I might have sex someday."

"By the way, I'm late." Nadine throws this tidbit in without warning. "What about you?"

My head pops up and I can feel my eyes getting wider. "What? Late? Are you pregnant?"

"No, please. I mean I haven't started my period yet. Like, ever."

"Oh, that sort of late." I calm down. "Sorry, but in this house being *late* is a biggie."

"Have you had a period yet? You've never said anything."

"No. I'm still waiting to 'become a woman' and be fulfilled." We both laugh. *It feels good to relax.* "Do you remember watching that video in fifth grade? So lame, did anyone take that video seriously?"

"My favorite was when the girl runs to her father and brags about entering the ranks of womanhood." Nadine shakes her head. "I can't imagine telling my father anything like that. It's bad enough having my mother asking every doctor what's wrong with me. Why I'm not more like Suzy-Q, Jenny-R, or Rachel-S? Their periods started when they were ten or eleven or twelve, something like that. I absolutely don't want to be like any of the QRS girls."

"So what do the doctors say?" I ask, hoping for details.

"Didn't I tell you this?" Nadine doesn't wait for an answer. "Some girls are naturally late. Because of sports, I lack enough body fat. My mom says I have to gain weight if I want to be 'normal.' As if normal's a real thing." Nadine shrugs. "What does your mom say?"

"My mother doesn't talk to me about any of this stuff."
I keep my eyes on my nails to hide my disappointment.
How am I supposed to become self-sufficient or feel safe?

"She didn't have 'the talk' with you?" Nadine sounds surprised.

"No. She gave Brendan a book about the human body when he started high school. He said he already knew everything except how to avoid zits. He read that part and gave me the book a week later. I read the whole thing, but I still don't know why my period hasn't started. And to make things worse, I can't get rid of the zit on my chin."

"That's nuts," Nadine says. "My mom was sitting at the kitchen table when I came home from school one day. She had a box of tampons and pads waiting for me. I got the feeling she was looking forward to giving me these *special* gifts and having 'the talk.' I almost died. Is it weird we are discussing being able to get pregnant and your Mom's going to have a baby?"

"Totally." I downplay my emotions. "Mom pretends to like me... until the truth comes out. I know she doesn't really, so I dodge her. Is it normal to avoid your mother? They're supposed to love you immediately, but that didn't work." *What's wrong with me? Oh yeah, I'm a girl, who's not as pretty as Brendan, and probably a bunch of other unlikeable things.*

"What about the day we were *not* sexting?" Nadine asks quietly. "What was that about?"

"Mom acts crazy, sometimes." *I feel bad avoiding the topic.*

"Well, your mom should love you. You're a great person." Nadine shakes her head. "My mom asked what I knew. I told her I'm aware of sex. But no period means I can't get pregnant. Mom says it's possible but only right before your first egg's released. It's too confusing so I said I wasn't going to have sex until I know more. Mom was relieved. She said we'd talk when I need information. She's more concerned about porn." Nadine blows on her glittery nails. "If you search for the word 'sex' you have to be careful. There is a lot of questionable stuff. Start with sites like safeteens.org. Just not when your parents are around."

"I can't search online," I complain. "My parents are paranoid about online access. Being teachers, they've seen all the problems and expect Brendan and me to repeat all of them. Our computer is for homework only and Dad checks the search history regularly."

"Well, you can come to my house and I can show you." Nadine smiles.

Yep, Nadine's a great friend. "Thanks."

"What about your Aunt Lily?" Nadine asks. "She seems fun. Can you talk to her?"

"No!" My head pops up. "She's unhinged." I shiver at the memory.

"Has she left?" Nadine's surprised. "I thought she was staying until the baby's born."

"Didn't I tell you? She left before school started. She only ended up staying three weeks." *There, one hand painted.* "She and Mom don't get along. Mom tries to seem perfect. Having Aunt Lily around reminds her of their shared genes. It's a pretty shallow pool. She needs a warning sign—No diving. Brendan says we should kiss the ground Dad walks on." I try to laugh. *See? There's nothing wrong with me.* "Crap, where's that nail polish remover?"

"Oh goodie, I hear bad words." Brendan enters my bedroom and plops into my beanbag. "What's crap? Let's dish, I want to hear all about it."

"Brendan, this is my room. There's no reason for you to be on this side of the house."

"I have a reason. I've gotta do laundry, Smart-one. The washer's outside your room."

"Well, you should knock before you come in." I hold

both painted hands up. *My nails are still setting so I can't pull him out of the beanbag.*

"Your door wasn't closed, Spaz." Brendan aims a fake grin at Nadine. "Nice nails, Parasite. What're you doing here?"

"Hello, Brenda." Nadine knows how to stay calm around Brendan. "Prepping for the dance tomorrow. Want me to paint your nails? I have a neon green that'd look lovely on you."

"No thanks, Nathan." Brendan matches Nadine's tone. "I have my own date routines."

"Really? Seems to me you only need to take your monthly shower."

I try to change the subject. "Who's your date?"

Brendan ignores me. "I don't expect you to understand, being... *girls.* You two need more time to prep for your big dates." Brendan glances at me. "Well, at least one of you has a big date."

"Brendan, I swear!" I jump up and pull him from the beanbag. *My nails are ruined.* "Get out!" I yell as I push him out of the door.

* * *

When the doorbell rings, I let Dad answer it. *I'm still worried about ruining the nail polish Nadine applied for me yesterday after my big nail failure.*

"Hi, Mr. Gurke." Nadine steps into the foyer. "This is my date, Jimmy Diya. Jimmy, this is Linn's dad, Mr. Gurke." Nadine breezes into the living room.

Dad uses his principal voice to stop Jimmy from following. "So, you're tonight's driver? Where and when did you complete your driver's education?"

I give Nadine a quick hug and tilt my head toward the front of the house. "Should we help him?"

"Don't worry, he's fine. This isn't Jimmy's first experi-

ence with a suspicious white guy. By the way, I've sched-uled a spa day for us. It can be used any time this year."
Nadine hugs me and whispers, "Happy Birthday, Linn."

"Thanks," I whisper back and wipe away the tears forming in my eyes.

Nadine looks me over. "That dress looks great on you. I told you an A-line style would be fantastic. We did well at Rent-A-Dress Depot! Plus, you'll get half your deposit back."

I glance around to see if Mom's nearby. "Be careful, Mom will lose it if I tell anyone we're struggling with mon-ey. And you look amazing too! Your mom can really sew."

"This little thing?" Nadine teases. "I picked the tra-peze dress pattern because it's so easy. But yes, she's a stitching goddess."

"Sure." I flash an exaggerated eye roll. "We won't talk about how the dress shows off those shoulders. Swim team is good for something. You were made to swim the fly."

"Well, distance isn't easy. You have to have patience to swim that far."

Our mutual admiration breaks up when the doorbell rings again. Dad moves to open the door and Jimmy es-capes into the living room.

I head toward the front door. "Alan's here, let's get going."

Jimmy looks at the foyer where Alan's having a friend-ly conversation with Dad. "Why isn't Alan getting grilled?"

"He doesn't have a driver's license." I'm watching Dad while speaking to Jimmy. "Your car's out front?" I step into the foyer, hoping the others will follow.

Dad stops us. "Oh, no you don't. You can't sneak out of here without pictures. I have my trusty camera ready to go." Dad turns and grabs the oldest camera on the planet. "Now line up and let me snap a few pics."

The four of us move into the living room.

"Scoot together," Dad directs. "Do you want to button up that shirt, Jimmy?"

Jimmy glances down at his attire. "What's wrong with my shirt?" he asks.

"The flannel shirt is unbuttoned and your t-shirt's showing." Dad's camera clicks.

"It's the new style, Mr. Gurke," Nadine offers. "The informal tee and unbuttoned cotton shirt balance the dress pants and jacket. It's called 'formasual' and it's all the rage."

"It looks like you forgot to button your shirt." Dad peeks out from behind the camera. "Us old people call that dementia."

"What do you think about my outfit?" Alan steps forward and strikes a pose. "Bow tie, dress shirt, dress pants, and snazzy suspenders."

"You'd be fine, Alan," Dad responds, "if your shirt didn't cause blindness."

"Dad," I complain. "Don't be rude."

"Don't worry, Linn." Alan beams at me. "I picked a red glitter shirt and black suspenders to match the dance theme, Ignite the Nite. I'm on fire."

"Somebody get the extinguisher," Dad mumbles.

I fake a smile and the camera clicks.

"Just a few more." Dad leans around the camera.

Mom appears in the foyer. She leans against the doorframe. Her upper lip's curling. *This is why I've been concerned all day. I lie because I don't want my friends to know about my unhinged mother. Will they still like me if they know the truth?*

* * *

After a few more camera clicks, I grab my clutch and urge my friends to move. *Somehow we avoided a 'mom in-*

cident.' Maybe the pregnancy's keeping her from drinking? Or is it because the tumbler's full of wine and not bourbon? Brendan's smart to meet his date at school.

My dread slips away as Jimmy drives toward the school. *Javy'll be there. He'll see me and ask me to dance. Our dates will be forgotten...*

"... right, Linn?" Nadine's waiting for confirmation.

"I'm sorry, what did you say?" I shake off my daydream.

"The dance. Ignite the Nite is the theme. Brendan says it's a play on the school name, Firestorm, right?" *Nadine still thinks my brain's in the car.*

"Yeah, Brendan says every dance he has attended used a fire theme." I stare out the window at the shops and houses. "Why do people think fire is funny or cute? I hate fire. I'm always afraid it's going to get me."

"If the fire doesn't get us, the earthquakes will." Alan shrugs "If you're going to live here you have to have a sense of humor about Mother Nature hating us. Might as well laugh and enjoy life while you can. YOLO!"

Jimmy shakes his head. "I'm dropping you two at the front of the gym. Nadine and I'll park the car and see you later."

Nadine turns in her seat. "If I don't see you inside, text me when you want to leave."

"Got it," I say as I slide out of the car.

Alan and I enter the gym to an overwhelming amount of crepe paper and balloons. Orange, red, and yellow streamers twisted together like fire, and small fans behind the fake flames, mimicking sparks rising into the night. Balloons hang from the streamers and a few move across the floor every time the door opens.

"Let's hope there isn't a real fire tonight," Alan whispers. "All this paper and helium. We'll go up like the Hindenburg."

Before I can thank Alan for his not-so-calming commentary, Ms. Garcia greets us.

"Hello, Linn, Alan. You both look fantastic." Ms. Garcia smiles at me. "I see you're fully dressed this evening. Let's keep it that way." She winks and moves to the next couple.

"What was that about?" Alan asks.

"I told you, I'm guilty of lewd and lascivious behavior. I took some clothes off."

Alan takes a half step away from me. "I didn't think you were serious. You're not going to take your clothes off tonight, are you?"

"If you don't behave, I'm going to get naked right here and rub *all* my goods on your body." I give Alan an evil look. "That's a threat, buddy."

Alan laughs. "Right, like you'd ever get naked in public. Come on, let's dance."

Alan watches way too many old musicals and can recreate most dance moves. All I have to do is follow his lead. For thirty minutes Alan shows off his shuffle steps, shimmies, bumps, and twists. *I'm the girl moving next to him. It doesn't require a lot of concentration and I study the crowd. There's Nadine and Jimmy. They have some good moves. Brendan's laughing with a group of girls. Which one is his date? Where's Javy? Who's he with?*

Alan moves close enough to get my attention. "Let's do the grass dance. You remember it's a simple two-step with the arm thingy I showed you."

I concentrate and we create a reasonable facsimile of the traditional Native American dance. People around us join in. The steps are easy to imitate and the music's an upbeat pop song. *I wonder if they realize this is a slow version of the warrior Pow Wow dance? Doubtful.*

Alan leans in and announces, "The DJ's going to play your favorite next."

"What favorite? My favorite song?"

"No, silly. Your favorite dance." Alan's in his element.

"My favorite dance? I'm confused. I don't know full dances, just a few moves."

"Sure you do. It's astounding." Alan waits for me to react.

"Alan, I only know the one..." My eyes widen in fear. "No, does anyone still do that?"

"We're about to find out." Alan pulls me to his side. "It's just a jump to the left..."

At that moment the DJ starts the "Time Warp" music. *I pray to the gods of dance Javy isn't watching. My pelvic thrusts need some practice. By the time we put our hands on our hips, half the student body's involved.* They're all ready to do the Time Warp, again. Brendan's dancing with a junior named Sonja. Nadine's dancing without Jimmy. Still no sign of Javy.

A round of applause erupts at the end of the dance. I smile at Alan but his head's swiveling from side to side. He mumbles something and leaves me standing alone on the dance floor. I turn to leave and bump into Steve Miller.

"Hey, Gurke. I see you saved me a dance."

Before I can react, Steve has his arms around me, and I realize why Alan took off. *Crap. It's a slow dance.* I wedge my arm between us so I can breathe and stop Steve from putting his head on my shoulder. "Enjoying the dance?"

"I am now." He attempts to pull me closer. "Even though you dumped me. You know I can't help the fact that my foot twitches on your chair. I try not to bother you in class."

After an exaggerated sigh, I remind Steve, "I didn't dump you 'cause of your twitchy foot. Alan and I already had plans and you have a date. Where's Emma?"

"After the Time Warp, she went to get punch. She's winded. I saw Alan leave the floor and figured you needed a little Steve love."

OMG, the ego on this guy! I use my wedged arm to break

our connection. "Emma has the right idea. I'm thirsty too. See ya later." I move toward the punch table as quickly as possible. I get in line and grab a cup as soon as I reach the front. *Deep breaths, relax. You ditched Steve. Maybe.*

As I raise the cup, a hand touches my neck. I squeal and the punch slops out.

A voice behind me whispers, "It's spiked."

I turn to find Javy standing there.

Javy stares at my punch-stained dress. "I'm so sorry. Did I cause that?" He grabs napkins from the table and advances toward the front of my dress. "Can we wipe it off?" He stops short, arm extended toward my chest, napkins in hand. His face reddens. "Um, here are some napkins."

I'm frozen in place and don't know what to do or say.

Javy breaks the silence. "Will you be able to fix the dress? It's great on you."

Great. Just great. Javy thinks my dress looks good with red punch stains! My brain kicks into Dad's science mode. "I don't know. I can't use bleach because it will ruin the flowers. Dish detergent won't hurt the flowers, but I don't think it will remove the stain on the white fabric. I could try white wine but that's a dangerous option if Mom's home." *Shut up. Stop talking!* "Maybe hydrogen peroxide." I can't stop the words from pouring out of my mouth. "It's only hydrogen and oxygen with a lot of water added. The bubbles are safe for cotton. I can't remember, what's color safe and will develop a covalent bond with the red dye in the punch? I don't think punch is an acid but I'm not sure if it's a base either." I finally stop talking and consider Javy hopelessly.

"Are you all right, Linn?" Ms. Hess arrives to check on us. "What's happening here?" She looks at my dress and the napkins still in Javy's outstretched hand.

"Just your typical dance conversation about covalent bonding," Javy quips.

Ms. Hess gently takes the napkins from Javy. "Thank you, Mr. Ramos. I'll take it from here." She turns her back on Javy. "Come with me, Linn. We'll see what we can do."

Ms. Hess leads me into the bathroom. The minute we enter, other girls hurry to leave. *There it is, the sound of Hess's walk causes fear in every student.*

She hands me some of the napkins. "Here, put these behind the dress. They will soak up some of the punch as you dab the front with water. Make sure it's cold so the stain doesn't set." I stuff my dress and begin to dab. Ms. Hess continues to hand me napkins. "How did you end up with punch all over and Javy looking guilty?"

"It was nothing." *I know I'm turning red.* "He surprised me, and I reacted poorly."

"Why did you react poorly to him? Is there a problem with Javy?"

How to answer? I decide on avoidance. "Javy says the punch is spiked."

"Happens every year." Ms. Hess chuckles. "Did Javy do the spiking?"

"No," I say too quickly. "I mean, I don't think he did it. I wasn't there. I didn't see. I don't know who—" *Shut up. You have got to control yourself at least once tonight.*

"Don't worry," Ms. Hess interrupts. "I don't think it was Javy. Besides, we have bigger issues tonight."

"Bigger issues?" I ask as I finish blotting. "Bigger than spiking the punch?"

"When you leave, go out the front door. The resource officers are out back dealing with a problem. It's worse than spiked punch." Ms. Hess isn't laughing any longer. "I think we've done what we can. Soak your dress in club soda when you get home." Ms. Hess turns and walks out.

I look at myself in the mirror. *There's a pink stain all over the front of the rented dress. It matches the color of my face. See? I'm not the fairest of them all and I forgot to ask*

Javy about his date. My outside's as damaged as the inside. Happy birthday to me. Not.

Nadine and Alan are waiting when I walk out. "What were you doing in there with Ms. Hess?" Nadine asks.

"And why do you look like a Popsicle that melted?" Alan adds.

"I'm fine. I spilled punch and Ms. Hess was helping me. Can we grab Jimmy and go home before the crepe paper begins to stick to me?"

"We have a problem." Nadine shakes her head. "Principal Greene thinks Jimmy was doing drugs. They don't have any evidence, but they called his parents, and he can't leave."

"Jimmy? Does drugs?" I'm beginning to understand Ms. Hess's warning.

"No," Nadine declares. "We were nearby, and Greene pulled just him into an office. Like I'm not dangerous enough to be questioned. They've also kept others and are calling their parents. I'm glad they didn't keep me. But Jimmy—"

"Yeah," Alan jumps in with his slice of gossip. "I saw a rent-a-cop showing Vick, Tony, and Maureen into an office."

"Do you think we could catch a ride home with Brendan?" Nadine looks around. "Jimmy texted and told me not to worry. He'll talk to me tomorrow."

"Brendan has to stay and clean up." I scan the gym. "That may take a while. I guess we'll have to call someone else."

Steve approaches. "Nice fashion statement, Gurke. Did you hurl or what?"

"Spilled punch, thanks for asking." I nod at Steve. "Trying to figure out how we're going to get home. Our driver's been delayed."

"You're in luck." Steve beams. "Emma drank a bunch

of punch and isn't feeling well. She's in the bathroom. I called my mom to pick us up. She should be here soon."

A few minutes later Emma joins our group. She gives Steve a small smile. "Sorry, I don't know what happened. I drank three cups of punch and felt woozy. Maybe I'm allergic."

I should tell her the punch's spiked, but I don't. I don't want to talk about Javy while I'm dressed as a sticky mess or any other time.

Steve looks at his phone. "Mom's here and parked out front. Let's go."

We head to the car. Steve and Emma slide into the front. The rest of us pile in the back.

"Thanks for coming to get us, Mom." Steve surveys the car. "Where's Billy?"

"I left him with your father." Mrs. Miller looks past Steve. "How're you feeling, Emma?"

"Okay, I guess," Emma moans and leans her head against the window.

"You left Dad with a six-year-old?" Steve asks.

Mrs. Miller glances at the back seat. "He's fine, Stevie. Are you going to introduce me?"

Steve waves a hand at the back seat. "These are my friends—Linn, Nadine, and Alan."

"I'm so happy to meet Stevie's friends." Mrs. Miller glances at us in the rearview mirror. "And, oh my, two such pretty girls. Good for you, Stevie."

"Mom," Steve whines, "please stop."

Alan leans toward me and whispers, "I'm pretty too."

"Of course, you are," I murmur in response.

"Where are we going?" Mrs. Miller asks. "Can I get directions? Is that allowed?"

"Drop Linn off first," Steve replies in a soft voice. "She lives near us, so just head toward our neighborhood." He turns and asks, "Where should we take the rest of you?"

"I live near Emma," Alan announces. "I'll walk from her house. That way I can make sure she gets home in one piece."

"Thanks, Alan," Emma responds weakly. "You know where I live Mrs. Miller. It's just around the corner from your house."

"That leaves me," Nadine says. "I live in Walker Hills. It's near Mercado Plaza."

Steve nods his head and turns back. "Got it." He gives his mother directions to my house. I'm not surprised he knows where I live—we've ridden the same bus for years.

I relax in the back seat and consider what's wrong with me. Everyone except Alan wants to get home before Emma's stomach erupts again. He's the only person willing to help her. And that includes Steve, her date. What's stopping me from being helpful?

When I get home, I announce my return through Mom and Dad's closed bedroom door. Stripping my dress off, I put it in the laundry sink and add club soda. I grab my journal and list the pros/cons of the evening.

Pro – Mom didn't lose it

Con - Dad's picture taking

Pro - Javy ~~spoke to me~~ touched me

Con – I nerd rambled to Javy and Hess

Pro - Alan and I danced well

Con - Slow dance with Steve

Pro - Dress looked good at first

Con - Spilled punch, it's not coming out

Pro – Nadine and I are still friends

Con – Dress deposit money gone

Con – Dad will think Jimmy's a stoner

Con – wasn't honest with Emma

Con – Steve seemed worried about Billy

Total = Ignite the Nite was a disaster

* * *

Journal Entry – Birthday Dance Disaster

For a few minutes tonight, it felt like a birthday party. When I was dancing with Alan, I wasn't worried. Time Warp was a hit. So many people joined in. Alan and I were the leaders.

I'm not telling Mom about the ruined dress and lost deposit. Mom cares about money but she cares more about other things and it's not her child. Me, money, or booze... what matters most? If I sit in one room with her wallet and put a bottle in the other room—where would she go? She's definitely going for the liquor! I used to think Dad was her only love with Brendan a distant second. Now I think she loves alcohol more than anything or anyone. Definitely an idea that doesn't make me safe.

I keep thinking about the night. There was something wrong with Steve during the car ride. I mean, other than his mother driving us. My eye muscle felt like it wanted to twitch, so crazy stuff was about to happen. But I don't know what it was.

LEAP
5, Dating – Alan was a great date for the dance. He looked great all night. Okay, he's a safety date—not the same as a real date. Alan isn't interested in girls but he's not ready to be seen at a school dance with a guy. Besides, Alan says he hasn't found a boyfriend yet. Alan saved me from a fate worse than death—Steve. We decided to help each other. That's what friends do, right? I shouldn't complain. Steve would date me, but I'm not interested. I need to watch out for Steve and his slow dancing. That boy does <u>not</u> understand personal space.

Golden Boy noticed me. Actually, he noticed my boobs. But not because I took my shirt off. He must think I'm a walking set of yabbos. How do I convince him (or any guy) that I'm more than boobs? Find a guy who's not focused on my chest... other than Alan. Ha!

Linn

Walker

Gurke

Chapter 8
On the Fly

OCTOBER'S FINALLY HERE. I love it when the tree leaves change colors and the weather's cooler. This month has a lot going for it. Alan asked me to help at his next craft fair, the Key Club has a fundraiser, and Brendan is planning his choices for our yearly Fright Fest. He and I have been doing Fright Fest since I started sixth grade. I was old enough to see horror shows then and we've made it an annual event ever since. It's going to be a month of fun! But first, I'm going to lounge in my warm bed with a blanket pulled up to my nose, 'cause it's Saturday and I don't have a schedule.

"Get up, Linn," Mom shouts through my door. "Tomorrow's your father's birthday and you need to help." Unfortunately, I'm wrong about today. I forgot about Dad's birthday and it's not going to be one of those days.

I'm not allowed to lock my door. Why doesn't she come in quietly and wake me up with a gentle touch? Oh, yeah, Mom doesn't have a tender bone in her body—never mind.

"Ugh." I cover my head with the pillow. "Ten more minutes," I beg.

"I let you sleep until eight." Mom's still yelling at my door. "On the farm, I had to feed the chickens and collect eggs before seven or my father punished me for being lazy."

This isn't a farm... Your father was a... Keep your mouth

shut. "Okay!" I shout back.

When I stumble out of my room, Brendan's sitting at the breakfast table eating cereal.

"Happy Saturday, Spaz," he says without lifting his head.

"Nice hair, dude," I respond. "You need to wave a brush over that mop."

Mom puts a box in front of me. "Eat some breakfast. I need you both to help with your father's birthday." She stands back and rubs her baby bump. "We need groceries for his dinner. I'm getting too big to drive. You two need to help shop."

My birthday gets canceled, but I have to smile and create a party for Dad?

"You could give me a list and your credit card," Brendan suggests.

"You aren't old enough to buy everything I need." Mom smirks. "The dinner menu is a surprise. I don't want to discuss this with your father in the other room."

"Brendan can drive. Why do I need to go?" I ask.

"Is it so difficult for you to help once in a while, Linn?" Mom's voice's getting higher, a sign she's losing control.

"No," I mumble. "I'll get dressed and grab my shoes." I remember Brendan's advice—don't move into Mom's blind spot and cut into her perfection lane. *I'm a perfect child... My mother has perfect children...*

"Eat your breakfast first," Mom yells.

I bolt down some cereal and get dressed in a hurry. *Let's get this over with.*

"We need liquor and groceries," Mom announces once we have settled in the car.

Brendan peers at Mom. "Liquor?"

"Yes, Brendan." Mom's upper lip is curling. I know a lie is nearby. "We're making your father's favorites. That includes grasshopper pie so we need crème de menthe and crème de cacao. Where else can we buy those?"

Nope. Dad's favorite is apple pie. I can think these things but I shouldn't say anything. I'm a hostage in my own family. Can't leave, can't speak, can't scream out loud. Screaming in my head doesn't make me feel better.

Ten minutes later Brendan pulls into a parking spot and turns the car off. "Which store should we start with?"

"Let's not waste time," Mom says. "We'll go to the liquor store first. You can bring the bottles back to the car while Linn and I get groceries."

"Okie dokie, let's not be poky." Brendan steps out of the car and lowers his head. He hurries toward the Guzzling Grizzly liquor store.

"Mom, do you want a shopping cart to lean on?" I ask as I watch her struggle to keep up with Brendan.

"No. There's nothing wrong with me," she snaps and picks up her speed.

Of course, nothing's wrong. Except for being the oldest preggo in town. Sorry, I asked. When I enter the liquor store, Brendan has a basket and is walking toward the aisle marked 'liqueurs and cordials.' Mom's right behind him.

"Here we go," Mom says as she picks up a 750ml bottle of green crème de menthe and hands it to Brendan.

"Mom," I call from the front of the store. "They have smaller individual bottles of the same thing up here." I hold up a couple of the small bottles hoping she'll do the reasonable thing. "We could buy one or two of these and have enough."

"Put that back, Linn," she responds. "You don't know the recipe. I do. Besides, that's the clear kind. The pie's supposed to be green."

"Here's the crème de cacao," Brendan says as he puts another 750ml bottle in his basket.

Brendan brings the basket to the front counter.

"You've got to shut it, Linn," he whispers.

"Gonna need your ID, dude," the man behind the counter says. "I don't think you're old enough to buy alcohol."

"Mom?" Brendan asks as he looks around. "What're you doing?"

"Your father wants me to pick up the basics," Mom responds as she carries another 750ml bottle to the front.

"Do you think you should buy that size bourbon? You're pregnant," Brendan points out.

"It's for your father. But you're right." Mom returns the bottle to the bourbon section and reaches for the shelf above. "I can get this brand for nearly the same price." Mom grabs the larger 1.5-liter bottle and brings it forward.

"But Dad drinks gin, not bourbon," Brendan states.

Mom's upper lip is completely curled. "I don't need your advice."

Brendan shakes his head.

Obviously, neither of us wants to stand between Mom and a bottle.

"Looks like you have the situation under control, Brendan. I'll shut it and get started on the groceries while you carry your three liters to the car. If my conversion rate is correct, that's just shy of a gallon." I walk past the counter and head to the store.

* * *

"Linn, help me carry the bags," Brendan says as we arrive home.

"Leave the liquor bottles on the counter," Mom directs. "I'll take care of them. You two put away the groceries. Tomorrow's a surprise for your father's birthday, don't say anything."

So, he didn't 'ask for the basics.' How many lies will Mom tell today?

"Hey, guys." Dad jumps up as we drag the shopping

bags in. "Did you get anything special? Something for a birthday?"

"Don't be nosey, George," Mom says. "And stay out of the kitchen."

"That's me, Curious George." Dad reaches for one of my bags. "Sure you don't need any help, Linn?"

"No, thanks." I attempt to deflect his attention. "Which baseball game are you watching? Is that the Giants playing? Who are they playing?"

"The Braves, it's the brains vs. bravos. Today is the seventh game in the National League Championship series. Winner goes to the World Series," Dad replies as he returns to the television. "I'm betting on the brains."

"And they have brains because why?" I ask.

"We have Berkeley and Silicon Valley. It's obvious."

I turn away so he doesn't see my eye roll. "Good to know." *The logic of his statement escapes me, but I don't want to talk baseball today—should I tell him about buying too much liquor? That'd be a great birthday weekend.*

Mom's already filled her insulated tumbler with 'the basics.'

"I'm tired. Make sure you put all the food in the right place." Mom leaves the room.

"Sure," Brendan responds in a quiet voice.

* * *

Sunday morning starts as a weird replay of yesterday.

"Get up, Linn," Mom shouts. "It's your father's birthday. You need to help."

"Ugh," I repeat my new morning routine and cover my head with the pillow. *Today I remember not to ask for more time.*

"Don't be lazy. It's eight o'clock," Mom yells.

Don't say it, Linn. Don't say it.

"Okay," I shout. "I'm coming."

When I stumble out of my room, Brendan's sitting at the table eating cereal, again. And Mom's standing nearby, again.

Brendan looks up at me. "Welcome to Sunday. New day, same time, same breakfast, still a Spaz."

I sit down without comment and pour some cereal.

"Happy birthday to me, happy birthday to me." Dad enters the room singing. He walks up behind Mom and puts his arms around her. "What exciting plans do we have for today?"

Brendan and I wait for Mom to speak.

"We're making a special dinner," Mom says. "I have recipes for everyone, except you, George. You can watch football. Or is it baseball? I can't keep track. We'll take care of everything."

"How many people are we cooking for, Mom?" I ask. "Are your friends, the Kaplans, coming over?"

"No—just the four of us," Mom replies. "Besides, your father's birthday doesn't have to include other people to be special, Linn. Our family should be enough."

Again. I can't say anything right. "I didn't mean... I was..." Brendan walks out of the room. *Thanks for nothing, Bro.*

"Go get dressed. You need to help cook. Even if dinner's only for us," Mom scoffs.

Twenty minutes later Brendan and I gather in the kitchen. Mom's wearing an apron and flipping through her recipe cards. "Okay, here are the assignments."

Does she ever stop talking like a teacher?

"Brendan, you have three assignments," Mom continues in her teacher voice. "You've got the barbecue sauce, salad, and grilling. You should make the sauce first. While it cools, you can cut the lettuce and veggies. Then clean out the grill. Here are the recipes for barbecue sauce and green goddess dressing. Make sure the chicken will be ready at six o'clock."

"Why am I making barbecue sauce and salad dressing? They sell both of those at the grocery store," Brendan points out.

Mom considers Brendan for a few seconds before responding. "How lazy would I be if I bought everything at the store? Besides, this is going to be a special, home-cooked meal."

Brendan takes his recipes and heads to the fridge without further comment.

Mom turns to me. "Linn, you only have one recipe but it's complicated. You're making the grasshopper pie. I've cleared the top shelf in the freezer. The pie should go into the freezer by four but it would be better if you put it in sooner. Once you've got the pie in the freezer, you can wash the dishes. I ran out of dish soap and forgot to pick some up at the store. Use the laundry detergent I've put in the measuring cup by the sink."

"Okay." I check around for Brendan. "I call dibs on the food processor and the good liquid measuring cup."

"Both of you," Mom raises her voice. "Pay attention."

I freeze halfway to the cabinet. Mental eye roll, mental snap to attention and salute, mental scream. Why does she think we aren't paying attention every time we joke around?

"I'll be making bread in this area." Mom indicates the counter between the sink and the stove. "Brendan, you have the stovetop and the counter near the fridge. Linn, you can work in the area from the sink to the doorway. Get all your ingredients out before you start. Do all the measuring first. Put each item away after you use it. It's the only way to keep the kitchen clean."

Brendan and I look at each other. Brendan gives me a zipped lip sign behind Mom's back and moves around her enlarged belly to collect his ingredients. Brendan creates a pile of onions, parsley, and vinegar. *I get all the stuff a*

*growing girl desires—chocolate, Oreos, marshmallows, and
liquor.*

"Mom, is this the crème de menthe we bought yesterday?" I ask as I hold up the bottle. "This one's open and
some's missing."

She scowls at me. "Get to work, Linn. I don't have time
to deal with you."

Shut it, Linn. Don't speak the truth, Linn. I begin to
count Oreos into the bowl. Brendan slides up behind me
and snags a cookie. I pop one in my mouth also.

"Don't sneak the cookies," Mom says. "You won't have
enough for the pie."

*And this is different than the missing liquor, how?
Explains why I'm a liar—practice. Or is it because I live with
people who model this behavior?*

* * *

By one o'clock I'm ready for a break and some lunch.
I place my pie on the empty shelf in the freezer Mom
cleared for me.

"Pie's almost done," I announce as I exit the kitchen
and enter the breakfast area. "I've set my alarm for three
hours. That should get it good and frozen." I sit down and
begin to make a sandwich from the fixings on the table.

"Good," Mom says. "The bread's rising by the stove
and I've put my dirty dishes in the sink. After you eat
lunch, Linn, start washing the dishes. In an hour I'll punch
down the dough and shape some into rolls. The rest can
be loaves."

"The barbecue sauce, salad, and dressing are ready,"
Brendan adds. "I've also left some dirty dishes for you,
Linn." He smiles at me. "After lunch, I'll start cleaning the
grill. Then I'll be ready to cook the chicken."

"Ahhh, you're grilling chicken." Dad smiles at Brendan
as he enters the room. "Make sure you put some alumi-

num foil down first. Do you know where the chimney is to get the charcoal started? Use a sheet of old newspaper from the garage to help light the chimney. You'll only need one match to start the fire. Then bank the coals to one side on the foil. That'll make it easier to clean up. Remember not to let the coals get too hot. Put the chicken on the grill that isn't directly over the charcoal."

"I've got it, Dad." Brendan rolls his eyes.

"Yes, but cook it indirectly," Dad continues. "If you do it right, it will take a little longer but the chicken will be juicer. Remember not to turn the pieces too often. Or they dry out."

"Dad, I've done this before." Brendan switches topics. "What game are you watching? Is it the Giants?"

"No, today I'm checking out the 49ers," Dad replies enthusiastically. "They have a new wide receiver. The pundits say he's destined for the Hall of Fame. I want to see how he performs."

"Who are they playing?" Brendan asks.

"Seattle Seahawks. They have the uniforms your Mom doesn't like because of the green highlights." Dad grabs a sandwich and turns back toward the living room. "There's also a golf tournament on today. I'm going to switch back and forth. If you've got time, come watch with me."

"Sounds like a plan." Brendan stands up and collects his food. He turns to Mom. "I'm going to watch with Dad while I finish my lunch. Then I'll get back to work."

"My children are useless," Mom grumbles.

Useless? What have we been doing all day? Best to get out of her sight. Even doing dishes would be better. I take my sandwich into the kitchen.

I lean around the corner, back into the dining room. "Mom, where did you say you put soap for the dishes?"

"In the measuring cup by the sink."

"I don't see a measuring cup."

"Do I have to do everything myself?" Mom pushes out of the chair and walks into the kitchen. She moves the cooking utensils around on the counter. "Where did you put the soap?"

"I didn't touch the soap." I pick up an empty measuring cup from the dirty dishes piled in the sink. "Oh crap, was it in this?"

"Linn, what did you do?" Mom's voice begins to rise.

"I didn't do anything. I used the glass measuring cup for the pie. I never touched *this* one until right now."

We both look around the kitchen. Mom focuses on the rising bread dough.

"No, no, no." Mom begins to tap her forehead rhythmically with her finger.

"I'll check. I'm sure there's nothing wrong with the bread." My voice has moved up an octave. I pinch off a piece of the uncooked dough and pop it into my mouth.

It tastes like soap. Don't panic. Stay calm and maybe Mom will relax. *Try to tell her without making it sound like she made a mistake.*

"The soap's in the bread, Mom. Don't worry, I'll help you make new bread. We can fix this before dinner." I give Mom a hopeful smile.

"No, no, no. It's ruined." She moans. "You're a terrible cook. I need a drink."

Mom grabs her insulated tumbler, turns to the fridge, and pushes the ice dispenser. Nothing happens.

"Why doesn't anything work in this shitty house?" Mom pulls the freezer open and reaches for the ice bin.

The jerking movement rocks the entire fridge. As Mom reaches in, the grasshopper pie slides toward the front of the shelf, pauses for a moment then falls toward the floor. I reach out but I'm too far away to stop it. My sticky creation hits Mom's shoulder and lands wet side down on the floor.

"No, no, no, grasshopper." Mom begins to cry.

"Did you know grasshoppers can fly? They have wings." *Why does my brain think of lame crap when I'm stressed?* "And they can spit." Facts keep coming out of my mouth.

Mom turns on me. "You ruin everything. I can't do this again." She turns, walks through the gummy green catastrophe, and heads for the garage.

Dad comes to the kitchen door. "What's going on?"

"There's soap in the bread and the pie fell on the floor," I answer. "It could be called locust pie. Locusts are the same as grasshoppers. People don't want to eat anything called locust pie." *Is it possible to have diarrhea of the mouth? Obviously, it is for me.*

"Linn," Dad's using his teacher voice, "where's your mother?"

"She went to the garage. I think she's in the car. You can follow her green footprints."

"I'll talk to her." Dad turns and walks out.

"Holy shit, Linn. What did you do?" Brendan asks as he takes Dad's spot in the kitchen.

"Nothing. Mom put soap in the bread and opened the freezer. My pie jumped."

"Geez, Linn." Brendan turns and heads toward a noise in the garage. "Do you hear that? Mom's shouting at Dad."

I follow and we stop short of the garage door.

"Shush," Brendan whispers to me. "Listen. I think they're in the car."

We can hear the argument through the door. The words are muffled but understandable.

"This family's horrible," Mom screams at Dad. "Why am I stuck with children who can't do the simplest things? I'd be better off without any of you."

"You don't mean that, Bella." Dad's soft voice is harder to hear.

"I do mean it. And now I'm having another little shit," Mom sobs. "I'd be better off dead. I'm going to drive this car into a wall and kill us both. Then you'll be sorry."

"You're not going to do that, Bella." Dad's voice is getting stronger.

"I will. I'll kill this parasite and myself at the same time. Then we'll see. You don't care. You don't love me."

"No, Bella. I do love you. But if you kill yourself, you will not see what comes next. You'll be gone. That's it. You won't be watching from above," Dad shouts.

"No, no, no," Mom screams. "I'm going to drive into a wall and kill the baby. It's the only thing you care about, and I'm going to take the little shit away from you."

"You're not going to drive anywhere." Dad's voice sounds sad. "You forgot these. You can sit here all day if you want but I have the keys. I'll make you a drink, but it's my birthday and I'm going to finish watching the game."

Brendan and I scamper back to the kitchen when we hear Dad open the car door.

Dad walks into the kitchen where we are attempting to act normal. He steps around the mess on the floor and picks up Mom's insulated tumbler. "Linn, do what you can to clean up." Dad pours some bourbon into the glass and turns to Brendan. "Can you please continue with the chicken? We are going to have a birthday dinner tonight, no matter what."

"Sorry, Dad," I mumble. "I didn't mean to ruin your birthday."

"It's not your fault, Linn. I'm not angry. I'm sad. Sad about how much your mother suffers. Her father told her she had to be perfect. She doesn't allow herself to make mistakes. On top of it all, this pregnancy's difficult. We all need to do what we can to make the next few months easier." He looks at the tumbler and adds some water to the bourbon. "Whatever it takes. She'll be in soon. She has to pee every twenty minutes." Dad walks back toward the garage.

I turn to Brendan. "Do you think Mom will commit suicide or kill the baby?"

"No." Brendan's forehead wrinkles with thought. "I have my keys and Dad has his. Besides, I don't think Mom has the energy to drive."

"We should do something." I feel the tears building. "Call someone. We could call the suicide prevention number. I've seen it on the bathroom walls at school."

"Absolutely not!" Brendan hisses. "Don't you listen to anything? If you tell anyone Mom's having a problem, she'll have a complete meltdown and kill herself for sure. Mom needs to believe she's perfect. Watch, if we do nothing, tomorrow she'll act as if today didn't happen."

"We have to do something," I mutter. "This is a complete meltdown."

"We need to help Dad. If it weren't for Dad, this family would be an f-ing disaster." Brendan shakes his head. "It's his birthday and Mom's batshit crazy. We need to finish this dinner and help Dad feel normal."

We really should do something before it's too late for the baby. Am I deluding myself into thinking I can do anything? Be realistic, Dad's living in denial. Brendan thinks we should pretend everything's fine—perfect, just perfection. No one's on your side, Linn.

"Okay." I shake off the tears. "The bread and the pie are dead. There's not enough time to redo anything. Can you go buy some ice cream? Or a cake?"

"Yeah, my car's out front." Brendan shakes his head. "What about bread?"

"Mom hates store-bought bread." I stare at the ruined dough. "Besides, that would remind her of soap-infused food."

"Let's not talk about the mistakes Mom can't handle.

Let's just stick with the idea you are solely responsible for our murdered dinner." Brendan's back to snarky. "When I have my own TV show, I'll call this episode—Death by Detergent. Besides, Mom always blames you."

Okay, Brendan. You want to pretend everything's normal. I'll play but only today. Not sure I can do this forever.

"Watch it, Sherlock." I stare at Brendan. "I didn't put the soap in the bread. But, I'll start cleaning the kitchen. You buy some ice cream and potatoes. I can cook potatoes."

"True. Potatoes have built-in defenses. They hide underground. Unlike your flying pie." Brendan gives me an evil grin. "You didn't kill my salad too, did you? By the way, next year we should consider buying Dad something he can record his sports on."

"I'm still trying to survive this year," I moan. "Either help me or get out."

"Hand me the foil, Spaz. I have to continue with the only part of dinner that isn't ruined. Then I'll run to the store."

Focus on cleaning the kitchen. When it comes to Mom, Brendan isn't your friend. You're alone.

* * *

I check my phone for the fifth time, almost midnight. It's still Dad's birthday. I can't wait for this day to be over. October has started off less positive than I thought. I pull myself into a ball and wiggle as far into the bed as possible. I open Snapchat and type a message to Nadine.

ME: you up?

NADINE: Yeah?

ME: bad day

ME: mom

NADINE: calling now

I know my phone's set for silent but I answer before the first vibration is over.

"Hey."

"Linn, what's wrong?"

"Dinner. Detergent ended up in the bread and the pie fell on the floor. Mom lost it."

"What do you mean, lost it?"

I open my mouth but my voice's failing. I whimper around my tears. "Mom... Mom... said she'd kill... baby."

"I'm coming over. I'll call Jimmy, we'll come get you."

"No," I whisper. "That'll only make it worse." I gulp down some air and wipe my nose on the pillowcase. "Everyone's asleep now. I just need to talk."

"I'm here." Nadine's voice cracks. "I'm always here for you."

"I know. I've been a bad friend and haven't told you everything. I don't want to hurt you, or my family. I don't know what to do."

"Can you talk now?"

I sob into my pillow, knowing Nadine's still listening. "I'm a mess... talk tomorrow?"

"You sure I can't come get you?"

"Yeah... no... I mean... don't come."

"We're supposed to make cookies at my house next weekend but that's too late. I'll meet you at school as early as possible and we'll make a plan."

"Okay." I let out a long sigh. "Sorry."

"Don't apologize, Linn. You know I love you, right?"

"Thanks for being my friend."

I hang up before Nadine can tell me not to thank her. The house is quiet but I can't sleep. I creep out of bed, grab my journal, and climb back under the blankets to write.

* * *

Journal Entry — Will Baby and I Survive Fall?

Eight months and Mom is HUUUUGE, but only her belly. The rest of her is getting very skinny. I would be worried but that isn't the worst thing. Mom's absolutely bonkers. I thought everything was semi-okay but it's not. Drama Momma threatened to kill herself and the baby. What do I do with that? Brendan and Dad told me not to do anything. I'm not sure I can follow their advice. I have to do something, right? I feel so bad. Why can't I do anything? Another failure for Fault-line Linn.

LEAP
I'm concerned about 8, Being safe on my list. I mean, I'm still worried. I haven't figured out how to feel safe myself. Now I'm worried the baby isn't safe either. This is a life-and-death kind of unsafe for him. Does my LEAP list apply to the unborn? Can I grow up if the baby gets hurt? Does this mean I care enough to do something that might hurt me? For right now, no one's dead. Mom's staying in her room and not talking much. Both she and the baby are alive. So that's sort of safe, right?

No, safe isn't happening for me—or the baby.

Linn

Walker

Gurke

Chapter 9
Situation Normal

IT'S SO NICE TO get out of the house on a Saturday and away from all the tension that weekends bring. My eye begins to twitch and I have to admit I told myself a sort-of-lie. Yes, I am out of the house but I'm still very tense. It's been about a week since Mom threatened to kill herself and the baby. Brendan acts as if it never happened. Still, everyone in the house is wound tight. Being happy to spend time at Nadine's house is the truth. Escaping tension is a lie. Nadine and I talked at school and made a plan to search the internet for answers. But I feel strange talking about Mom to anyone. I roll my shoulders back, slap on a smile, and push the doorbell.

Nadine pulls me into a hug as soon as the door opens. "So glad you're here. Did you remember the cookie cutters?"

"Yes, at least the ones that don't scream Christmas. I brought circles, hearts, and gingerbread people. Those will work for October cookies."

"Cool. Mom and I bought the ingredients. Come in, we can get the dough started." Nadine looks outside. "How did you get here?"

"Brendan dropped me off."

"Is he coming back for you later?"

"He's on his way over to Javy's house. He'll pick me up later. He needs me to watch horror movies with him. October means Fright Fest, remember? We watch one movie every day of the month. Brendan and me, of course."

I walk into Nadine's house. She lives in a neighbor-hood where the builder used five different floor plans. Their house is one of the two-story designs with a wrap-around porch. My favorite room is the kitchen. It's large with shiny appliances and a marble-topped island on one side. The rest of the space has an oversized farmhouse table near a bay window. Basil, chives, and thyme grow on the bench built into the window. I love sitting there breathing in the aroma.

"Hi, Mrs. Thomas," I greet Nadine's mother as she un-loads groceries. "Thank you for letting us make cookies for the Key Club's fundraiser. We'll clean up after ourselves."

"You're welcome, Linn. I'm so glad you talked Nadine into joining the group. In high school, I was a member of the Debate Club and Mock Trial. Our side always won."

"*Mom*," Nadine draws out the word as she protests. "Old history. Seriously old history."

"Yes, dear. And you'll be old someday too. It'll be fun." Mrs. Thomas removes the last item from her shopping bag. "I don't think I've ever bought shortening before."

"I'm sorry," I say. "Normally we only make these for Christmas. Mom says it's one day a year and Dad loves them. Pretty much everybody loves this recipe."

"Don't be sorry, sweetheart. You're fine." Mrs. Thomas pats me on the back.

I have no idea how to react to a nice Mom. "Okay, sorry." *Hold still and the kind lady might ignore me.*

Mrs. Thomas picks up her car keys. "You girls have fun. I have to take your sisters to the roller rink. Another birthday party! Remember, Nadine, with your Dad home no cookie's safe."

Nadine rolls her eyes. "I know. He's a walking garbage disposal."

I drop my plastic-sleeved recipe on the counter. "Let's

get the ingredients out, do all the measuring, and put things away as we use them to avoid mistakes." *I hate it when I sound like Mom. I hate it even more when she's right.*

Nadine looks at the recipe and opens the pantry. "Cool. So how are things going at your house this week. I mean, any more detergent mistake?"

"Mistake? That's the understatement of the year." I take the baking soda Nadine hands me. "Mom hasn't threatened to kill herself since last weekend. That's positive, right?"

"I'm so sorry, Linn. What can I do to help?"

"Do you have a few bowls? We're going to need one for mixing and another for dry ingredients."

Nadine opens a cupboard and starts pulling out bowls. "You were freaking out when we talked at school. It sounded like things were pretty bad."

"They were." I let out my breath, stopping the tears fighting to come out, and prepare to tell the truth. "I was scared. No. I *am* scared. But today's better, maybe." *Chicken. What other names can I call myself? Drama queen. Liar.* "If you mix all the dry ingredients in that bowl, I'll start creaming the shortening, sugar, and eggs."

"How much better?" Nadine asks as she measures out the flour.

"Dad bought some liquid dish soap and put it by the sink. Measuring cups are for food only from now on." I laugh but it doesn't sound normal. "I haven't seen Mom much. She's on maternity leave from teaching but is in her bedroom, a lot."

Nadine stirs the dry ingredients together. "So, you're hoping she doesn't get mad again."

"The baby needs to get here soon. Mom should feel better once he's born." I stop the mixer so I don't have to shout over the sound. "Okay. Start adding the dry stuff a little at a time and I'll pour in the milk."

After a couple of dry-wet cycles, I continue. "Let's admit it, my life's a mess and there's no fixing it."

"SNAFU!" Mr. Thomas walks into the kitchen and checks our bowl. "What're we making?" He sticks a finger in the bowl and licks off the dough.

"Dad!" Nadine pushes him with her hip. "There's raw eggs in it. You'll get sick."

"Multiple tours in the Gulf, honey, and the forces of evil haven't gotten me yet. I don't think a raw egg is how I'm going out."

"What did you mean by 'snap you'?" I ask.

"SNAFU? It's an old military acronym. It means Situation Normal, All Fucked Up."

"*Dad*," Nadine complains. "Language! There are small children in this house."

"I was telling Linn what SNAFU stands for. I heard her say things were a hopeless mess. We call that SNAFU. We expect the world to be all fu— I mean fudged up. That's why we say it's normal. Is there anything we can do to help you, Linn?"

"Thanks, but no." I give Nadine a warning look. "I'm fine, really." *There I go again, lying. My knee-jerk reaction to adults in the room—lie.*

"Dad, we're baking. So, you might want to—I don't know—watch television?"

"I get it, juvenescence-space needed. Let me know when cookies need tasting."

When Mr. Thomas leaves, Nadine turns to me with her hands on her hips. "I know you don't want to talk about your mom, but why? My parents could help. Somebody needs to do something before your mom, or the baby, gets hurt."

"I'm scared. If Mom or Dad find out I've told anything, they might kick me out of the house. Where would I go?"

"You could come here. You're welcome anytime."

"I don't belong here. Your family's great, but I need to stay home and help keep everything calm. Besides, I couldn't leave Brendan alone. He needs me."

"Linn, you love Brendan!"

"No! I just think Brendan needs help. He's more damaged than you know. I'm stronger."

"I hate to tell you, Linn, but you're not that strong. We talked about this at school, remember?"

"Yes," I admit. "This dough needs to sit in the fridge for at least forty-five minutes. I'll set an alarm. Then can I use your computer to search for information?"

"Sure." Nadine grabs the plastic wrap. "Let's get this stuff cooling."

"I don't want you to be in trouble. Will searching sites about suicide be okay?"

"Don't worry! I have my own computer and I know how to clear my search history."

I can't imagine having that kind of freedom.

Thirty minutes later I lean back from Nadine's computer, exhausted. Nadine's sitting on her bed hugging one of her stuffed bears. She has a death grip on the one with the Air Force uniform. *I wish I had a bear to hug right now.*

"Thanks, again, Nadine. I don't feel safe looking at this stuff at home or school."

Nadine sits forward. "No problem. Did you learn enough?"

"Are you kidding? I've learned too much. I don't know where to start."

"Let's start with the basics. What do you think is the most important fact here?"

"Well, it's good to know I can call any day or any time for help. That's if I'm ready to run for my life because Mom would kill me." I reconsider my word choice. "I mean— she'd freak out."

"What about your dad?" Nadine asks. "Why doesn't he

do anything?"

"I have no idea. He covers for Mom. The other day he said he felt sad because she suffers. But, he doesn't see Brendan and me suffering. I want to trust Dad."

"But you don't?"

"No. He says everything's okay. And he can take care of it. But..."

"But what if he can't?" Nadine stands and comes closer to me.

"Yeah, what if he can't? And what if he won't? It's all so confusing."

We both stare at the computer for a long moment, hoping it will give us different answers. I sneak a look at Nadine. Her mouth is pulled into a frown. I know my face must mirror the confusion I see in Nadine. We both sigh at the same time. I attempt to stifle a laugh and end up snorting.

Nadine turns and points out, "You snorted."

"We had a synchronized sigh. That was snort-worthy." I turn back to the computer. "Okay, check out this page."

"Is there anything helpful there?" Nadine asks.

"A little. This site lists the signs and symptoms of suicidal people, Mom doesn't fit the description. At least not every symptom."

"What do you mean?"

I point at one of the websites. "Mom does talk about killing herself, but she seems to think she'll be around to see the results. She doesn't say she's hopeless. Instead, she says Dad doesn't love her and she's going to punish him."

Nadine leans down to see the computer. "But those things are on the list. Sort of."

"Yes, at the top. But look down farther. Mom isn't making a plan. She ran out to the car and didn't even take the keys. She doesn't feel shame. After all, she believes she's perfect."

"Does she drink too much?" Nadine points to the website's list. "She acts out and has mood swings like someone who drinks."

I ignore Nadine's words. "It's like one of those logic questions. Two cars are traveling to Florida. Person A must always ride with person C. Person E can never be in the same car as Person A—blah, blah, blah. Who wants to drive to Florida with these people anyway?" I stand and move away from the computer. "To make things more confusing, Mom has threatened to kill herself before. I mean—is she actually a danger to the baby? I wish I could talk to a psychologist!"

"Still, it's good that you're talking to me." Nadine sits at her computer. "Here's a site that says some people with personality disorders threaten suicide. Does that description fit her?"

I feel bad that I still haven't told Nadine all the mean drunk parts of Mom.

"I've always wondered if Mom says these things to control Dad—and us. I don't know if she means what she says. That could be good."

"It could. But what if you're wrong?"

"Right, what if I'm wrong? I'd feel so guilty. It would be bad enough if Mom killed herself. I'd feel even worse if she killed the baby. Sucks, doesn't it?"

"Yeah, it does."

Nadine and I sit in silence until my alarm beeps.

"Cookie dough's ready." I stand and look at Nadine. "Let's go bake the cookies and make the icing."

We walk back down the stairs and into the kitchen.

"I'll roll and cut the dough out if you heat the oven and set the timer."

After sheets and sheets of cookies, we begin to make icing.

"Can you melt some butter? I'll get the mixer ready." *I*

smile, knowing I'm back in my element. I can control icing.

Nadine pulls the butter out of the fridge and places it in the microwave. "You shouldn't feel guilty. This isn't your fault. Are you going to call the prevention number?"

"Watch out, I'm putting the confectioners' sugar in the bowl. This stuff goes airborne and covers everything if you're not careful."

Nadine pours melted butter and milk in the bowl.

I add vanilla and turn on the mixer so I have time to think.

"What about the consistency?" I ask. "Food coloring will make it thinner."

Nadine watches blobs of icing drop from the beaters. "Seems good for now. Not too thin. The websites say you should take all threats seriously. So, will you call?"

"If you were the one threatening suicide, I would call. Your parents would step up and help you. Your family would stay together and work things out. But if I call about my mom, then what'll happen? I live with a bunch of liars. What if the police come to our house? They might break up my family. I would have to leave home. I don't care if Mom gets angry with me, but what about Dad? Teachers can't have this kind of issue. They'd both lose their jobs and the house. I'd be messing up more than my life. Brendan and I could be split up and sent to foster homes. He should be part of this decision, but Brendan's told me to shut the fuck up. If Dad would step up, then Brendan and I wouldn't have to make decisions like this. Yes, I have to grow up, but shouldn't my parents already be grown-up?" A shiver of fear runs down my body. *Thinking about my life is hard enough. Talking about it scares me.*

"What about Eric?"

I take a deep breath to calm down. "The baby doesn't get a vote until he's at least five." I check Nadine for a reaction. "Sorry, bad joke?"

"Linn, the baby will be here soon, and you still haven't said his name."

"A name would make him real." I eject the beaters from the mixer and tap them on the side of the bowl. "What if he doesn't develop? Or survive? I'm not ready for any of this." I lean against the island with the beaters in my hands. "I need to keep Mom from being upset."

"Why wouldn't he develop?" Nadine asks. When I don't answer, she continues, "You can't control this on your own, Linn."

"I can try. And I can be there for Brendan."

"And I will be here for you. Even if you don't tell me everything, I'm a friend." Nadine hugs me despite the messy beaters in my hands.

I close my eyes—don't cry... don't cry. Well, crap.

"Hey, guys. Break it up or get a room." Alan walks into the kitchen, takes a beater out of my hand, and licks it. "Yummy."

Nadine and I both wipe the tears away as we pull apart.

"Alan, what are you doing?" I sniff.

"Don't you remember? I'm helping with the cookies."

Nadine rolls her eyes. "How did you get in without using the doorbell?"

"Your Dad was outside," Alan says. "Point is, I'm here now. Doing my Key Club service in the form of cookies."

I pull my lips back in an attempt at happy. "It's good to have an artist decorate. Besides, you're the reason we joined the group, and we like having you around."

"I like being around. Now, what can I do?" Alan asks.

"Take a bowl, spoon some icing into it, and mix in some food coloring. I'll put one bowl aside for white icing and make the colors red and blue. Nadine can do green and yellow. Alan should do the colors that need mixing—purple, orange, and brown."

"Sure." Alan collects bowls of icing and sits at the table. "But that isn't what I was asking. When I got here, you were hugging and crying. What's happening and how can I help?"

"Nothing," I respond. "Everything's fine."

"Linn." Alan looks at me. "I'm not a complete idiot. I know you're lying. Nadine's a friend, I am a friend, talk to us. Tell us the truth."

Goosebumps form on my arms as I realize—I'm not alone. *I have friends. Plural.*

I nod in agreement. "You have to promise you won't repeat what I say. If Mom finds out I've been talking, I'm toast."

"Of course," Nadine agrees. "We won't say a word to your mom."

"Or Dad, or Brendan." I stop and think. "Or pretty much anyone."

"Got it." Alan mimics zipping his lips. "Keep it away from everyone."

We sit around the kitchen table decorating cookies. I tell my stories. *It's surprising how little time it takes me to unload years of... what? Blame, guilt, threats, and fear. Lots of fear.*

* * *

Nadine shakes her head. "I wish you'd told me... I mean... I don't know what I mean."

Alan shrugs. "I'm sorry to hear about this but I'm not completely surprised."

"Not surprised?" I ask. "What have you seen?"

"It's not about what I've seen. It's more like what I felt. The night of the dance things were going well. Your Dad started taking pictures, then your Mom walked in and you froze. The tension was crazy, and you were about to make a run for it."

"I was. We were lucky Mom didn't show us her crazy."

"I missed it," Nadine grumbles. "But you didn't feel that it was Linn's birthday."

Alan turns to me. "It was your birthday? Why didn't you say something?"

"Mom canceled my birthday and said not to tell anyone. Nadine knew because we've been friends for so long."

Alan looks me in the eyes and leans forward. "I'm sorry. If I'd known, I would have rented a limo or something."

"But don't you have to be older to rent a car?" I ask.

"That's the problem." Alan looks at us. "Age alone doesn't make you an adult. We give older people credit for being wise without any real proof. Take Linn's mom for instance."

"Yes, please. Take my mom!"

Alan ignores my attempt at humor and continues, "Based only on age, parents have all the money and make all the decisions. Why's that?"

"They work and make money," Nadine states. "We're in school and don't pay bills."

"I disagree." Alan stands up and moves some finished cookies to the parchment paper on the island. "I babysit so Mom can work and go to school. I don't get paid for watching my sister but neither does anyone else. If I keep us from paying for daycare, it's the same as making money. Shouldn't I be able to make decisions and have some power?"

"Your situation's different," I add. "There's only one parent. You help more than us."

Alan stares at me for a long moment. "Sounds to me like you only have one functioning parent at your house. There is you, Brendan, your dad, and an adult-aged, special needs child."

"And now that child's having a baby." Nadine frowns. "What will you do?"

I shrug. "Fifty decorated cookies later and I still have no answers."

Alan sits down and shakes his head. "Trust me, my ancestors have been asking what to do about alcoholism for generations. We still don't have a good answer."

"Do you have any bad answers?" I ask. "Any answer is helpful."

"Keep trying," Alan says. "It'll take more generations, but we've got to keep working."

"What are you working on, Alan?" Mr. Thomas enters the kitchen to check the cookies.

Alan crosses his eyes. "The cookies, sir. Do you want to try one?"

"Of course," Mr. Thomas responds.

"Go ahead and grab one," Nadine says.

Mr. Thomas picks up a cookie and flashes the front toward us. "This one's large and covered with Red Hots—quality and quantity. Yum."

"We better start bagging the cookies to get them away from Mr. Quality Control here." Nadine stands and heads for the pantry. "How many cookies should we put in each packet and how much should we charge?"

Mr. Thomas laughs. "These cookies are worth at least a dollar apiece." He grabs another and heads back to the living room, calling out, "Put me down for two dollars. I'm good for it."

Nadine sits with her head in her hands, muttering.

Alan laughs. "Two dollars for two cookies seems fair."

* * *

Journal Entry – Halloween Cookies

Our table at the Key Club fundraiser was a big hit. It was a couple of weeks before Halloween and everyone was ramped up for sweets. They loved our cookies. Key Club created a school-wide sugar high, and we walked away with over a hundred dollars.

Ms. Hess offered to buy the cookie recipe from me. She said I could name my price. Wow, she really liked those cookies! I said I'd send her the recipe for free. You have to be nice to your teachers, sometimes, right? Ms. Hess gave us five dollars as a donation.

<u>LEAP</u>
4, Alan is older and becoming self-sufficient. He's getting his driver's license over Christmas break. I'm more than a little jealous.

7 and 8, I have <u>friends</u>... at least two. But I don't feel safe or know what I should do. I should have answers, but I'm afraid. I should be brave and make good decisions, but I don't know how. To be brave... or make good decisions. I'm afraid my family's doomed because I'm broke and chicken.

I should have a cookie sale for me – Save Fault-line Linn!

Linn

Walker

Gurke

Chapter 10
Saturday in the Park

I KNOW I'M DREAMING but I can't wake up. It's the same dream I've had since I was six and Brendan gave me a stuffed tiger for Christmas. A couple of years later the tiger disappeared while I was at school. Mom probably took her to the Kindergarten Kill Room. Still, the dreams continue.

In my dream, the tiger climbs up the side of my bed determined to eat me. But this time it is different. There is a leopard lying on a tree branch overhead. "What are you doing?" I ask the leopard in my dream.

"Waiting for you," it replies as its tail twitches. "I know you need sleep but, you're late."

I wake and sit up in a panic and look at my phone. "Oh crap," I say to myself. It's Saturday and I promised Alan I'd help at his craft fair. I jump out of bed and push the blackout curtains aside. Yep, Nadine and Mrs. Thomas are parked outside, waiting for me. "Crap," I say one more time for no one's benefit. I pull on the clothes I left on the floor yesterday and grab a hairband and my tube of SPF-infused lotion from the top of my dresser.

Speed walking through the kitchen, I'm happy it's too early for anyone else to be awake and demand that I eat. I slip on a pair of shoes and open the front door as quietly as possible. I slide into the backseat. "Were you waiting long?" I ask.

"No." Nadine turns around and smiles at me from the

front. "I know you need sleep, so we gave you a few minutes. We didn't even honk and wake up the neighbors."

Now I understand that Nadine was the leopard in my dream. Relaxing in the tree with her tail twitching and thinking, *I'll understand you and give you a few minutes more of sleep. Still, I'm waiting, and I could pounce. But, why? I don't need to jump on you.* I look around the back seat as Mrs. Thomas pulls out of the driveway. "Where are the twins?"

Mrs. Thomas looks into the rearview mirror and smiles at me. "When D. J. is deployed, I don't have much time to myself. I intend to take full advantage of him being at home. That means he's watching the twins." Mrs. Thomas gives a small laugh. "Watching those two will be more like a test for D.J. He's survived warfare, we'll see if he can survive the twins."

"Can we get to the Rivermart in twenty minutes?" Nadine asks.

"Rivermart? You mean the crafts fair at River Park? Whoever names these things needs help. Or a better thesaurus." Mrs. Thomas turns out of the neighborhood and onto the main street. "Of course we can make it. No problem."

I like this car. There's no tension, lots of smiles, and no crazy. So different than my family. *But let's not talk about that!* I pull my hair back and use the band to create a ponytail. Twisting the hair, I tuck the ends under a part of the band, creating a messy bun. It's the best I can do without a mirror.

Nadine looks back at me while faking an innocent expression. "Have you ever considered cutting your hair short again? Like it was when we first met."

"Never!" I reply as forcefully as I can so early in the morning. "A messy bun will have to get me through today." I open my SPF lotion and begin to slop it onto my arms.

"That and SPF lotion. Count yourself lucky that you don't need this to survive a day in the sun."

"Are you kidding?" Mrs. Thomas blurts. "I make all my girls use that same lotion every day. White girls aren't the only ones who burn."

"Mom!" Nadine laughs. "Don't give away all my beauty secrets."

"Really?" I ask incredulously. "I've known you since elementary school and I'm just now hearing this?"

"A girls gotta have some secrets." Nadine looks out the window. "We're here. Let's go find Alan and see what he needs us to do."

The car pulls over near the entrance to River Park. "Thank you for the ride, Mrs. Thomas. I'm sorry it was such an early morning."

Mrs. Thomas waves me off. "Oh, my. This isn't early! The twins have to get up early every weekday to catch the bus. Saturday is just another day, and I get to check out Rivermart without my dynamic duo girls. I'll collect you two when the shopping and selling is over. Good luck, and have a great time. I'll see you later."

Nadine and I exit the car and begin to walk through the vendors setting up their sites. We pass potters, decorative bird houses, leather vests, extra large scarfs, and woodworkers. Finally, I see a tent with Alan setting out his jewelry. I wave and we head his way.

"Hey," I greet Alan as we arrive.

"What do you need us to do?" Nadine asks.

Alan points Nadine toward the display. "Could you make the jewelry look attractive? And thanks for helping. Being at a craft fair isn't the best way to spend your weekend."

"What about me?" I ask. "How can I help?"

Alan turns toward me and says loudly, "Can you be at the front and entice people into the booth? Maybe do some of the sells?" Then he steps closer and lowers his voice. "Linn, a couple of the women with stalls nearby have been hitting on me. Can you act like my girlfriend? I need help, a cover, and I don't want to insult these women."

"So, throw Linn in front of them?" I whisper before smiling. "I'll chum the waters and distract the sharks."

Before the Rivermart even opens to the public, I'm overwhelmed with admirers of Alan and his jewelry. At least three older women and one man from nearby booths come by to 'chat' Alan up. I step in front of them each time and do my best girlfriend impersonation. It involves a lot of winks and smiles thrown his way. I even guilt two of them into purchases. One woman buys a ring and the man picks out a pendant made from a kiln-fired spoon with walnut shells. I remind them it might be late October, but Christmas is just around the corner and presents will be needed.

Nadine is giving me looks, questioning looks. As the public enters the park and the booths get busier, she sidles up to me and mutters through her teeth, "What are you doing? At the dance you said Alan was a 'friend.' And Brendan said he wasn't a real date. So, what's going on?"

I look at the back of the booth where Alan is wearing safety goggles and working with a small torch to bend a fork. Turning back to Nadine, I whisper, "I'm keeping the needy older people away from Alan."

"You mean Cougars?" Nadine asks.

"Those. And what do you call the older men who hover around Alan?"

"Men?" Nadine asks. She's about to say more when our attention is drawn away by a shrill voice.

"Stevie, look. It's the pretty girls from the dance. And, they're selling jewelry."

Nadine and I both turn toward Mrs. Miller and her pointed finger.

"Oh, I am definitely looking at this booth!" Mrs. Miller hurries toward us, leaving Steve and his younger brother.

"Mom!" Steve draws his words out as he folds both arms over his chest. "Don't embarrass me in front of Linn and Nadine." He looks past us. "And Alan."

"That's right." Mrs. Miller smiles at us. "It's Linn and Nadine." She walks nearer as she looks me up and down. "Oh, honey. Those clothes look like you picked them off the floor. I could help you with ironing tips. A pretty girl like you should look your best. Like your friend Nadine, here."

If Mrs. Miller gave me a moment, I'd tell her that I did just pick these clothes off the floor, and I already know how to iron.

"Have you eaten any breakfast, Linn?" Mrs. Miller doesn't wait for an answer. "I can have Stevie and Billy run to the food court and get you some food."

"Mommm," Steve complains again.

"No, thank you, Mrs. Miller. I've already eaten." Okay, that's a lie. But she's driving me mad in the very little time she's been here. I glance around her in an effort to get Steve's attention. Maybe he can control her.

"Or I could buy you a brush for your hair. There is a booth with..."

I walk away from Mrs. Miller.

Steve is standing in the same place he's been since we first heard her shrill voice. Billy is right behind Steve's right leg. I mean right behind! I walk forward, lower myself, and try to talk to Billy. "Hey Billy. What do you think of Rivermart? Have you seen anything you want to buy yet?"

Billy glances up at Steve for permission to speak to me. Steve nods to him. Billy leans forward and whispers to me, "A car. The wood man makes a car with wheels that roll. It's blue."

"Oh," I gush. "That sounds so cool." I look up at Steve.

"We're going back there on our way home. That is, IF I can get Mom away from Alan's jewelry." Steve rolls his eyes. "Are women attracted to his looks, or his art?"

I decide not to answer and change the subject. "While you're here are you going to take Billy down to the river?"

Steve looks down at Billy and shuffles his feet before responding. "Are you mental? That is not a river. It's more like a canal. And, no, I'm not taking my brother to see a bunch of concrete with a trickle of water in it. Come on, buddy," he says to Billy. "Let's go look for more cars." Steve looks directly at me as he continues to speak. "Mom can find us when she's done looking at Alan... and his pretty things."

They turn and walk away. Steve with Billy still behind his right leg. As I turn back to Alan's booth, I consider asking Mrs. Miller why Billy is so shy. Then I get a look at her fawning over Alan's jewelry and decide not to engage her again. I return to Alan's booth. Ignoring Nadine and Mrs. Miller, I talk to a woman looking at the display about Alan's work.

By the time the public is finally leaving, I realize I haven't had much time to talk with Alan or Nadine. We've had a busy day. Nadine collected the money but I'm better at math and she asks me to double check her numbers. I turn to Alan. "After subtracting for the cost of the booth, we've got four hundred, seventy-five dollars and twenty-four cents. I assume you started with some money for making change. Still, I think it was a good day."

"Yes." Alan smiles at us. "It was a good day. Both of you should take whatever you want. It's the only way I can pay you. Our family needs the cash. But, with you two helping up front I was able to make more items to sell later."

"Alan," I argue, "you can't be giving away your items. That will cut into your profits."

Alan looks at me and raises one eyebrow. "Try to re-

member what I told you. I use stuff people would otherwise throw away. I don't have a lot of upfront costs."

"B-but you have to pay for the safety goggles, your
torch, that vise, and the booth itself," I stammer.

Rolling his eyes, Alan flaps his hand in my direction.
"Stop. Linn. You don't always have to be so exacting. Just
because you know stuff, doesn't mean it should be said.
Just make me happy and take a gift when it's offered. In
fact, it's not a gift. You earned whatever you pick and more,
so do it." Alan turns his back on me and starts to collect his
jewelry-making tools.

Nadine motions me over to one of the displays. "Here
are two bracelets that look alike. If we take those we'll always remember working together." She smiles at me.

I really like Alan's jewelry and the bracelets are made
of silver forks with the tines curled into different designs.
I pick one up gingerly and try it on. *Yes, this is amazing!* I
smile back at Nadine then turn to Alan with my wrist held
up. "Okay, Art-boy. I like this one and will be proud to wear
it." I turn back around before he can see the tears forming
in my eyes.

Nadine is admiring the way her bracelet catches the
lowering sun. "Alan, have you ever considered selling these
on the internet? I'm sure you could make some money. I
could help you with the photography and website."

Alan shakes his head at her. "Thanks. But I'm busy
enough right now. Maybe after high school."

Nadine shrugs and begins to fold a tablecloth. I join in
and soon the booth is empty again.

"Do you need a ride home?" Nadine asks Alan.

"No, thanks. Mom is picking me up after work." He
glances at his phone. "She's waiting in the parking lot.
How about you two?"

"Mom has worn herself out enjoying her day away
from the twins. She got to the parking lot an hour ago. Said

she'd just take a 'quick' nap. We'll probably have to wake her up from a deep sleep. The woman does NOT do quick." Nadine gives a small laugh and looks around. "Have we forgotten anything? Linn, do you have your SPF lotion? You've gotten a little sun. You are seriously a pale girl."

Alan and I answer "No" in unison and then laugh.

I feel my pocket to make sure I have the lotion. We all pick up boxes and head toward the exit.

* * *

I walk into the house smiling. Despite the redness on my nose, it was a good day. My smile vanishes as I hit the kitchen area. Dad is sitting at the table and Mom is in the kitchen.

"Well, look who's finally arrived home." Mom's lip curls as her belly bump shuffles toward me. She grabs my hand and holds it out for Dad. "While I've been making dinner, Linn has been collecting trinkets from her boy toy, Alan. And, what did you do to earn that?"

"I helped sell jewelry at the craft fair. I told you this."

"Of course, we believe everything you tell us," Mom says sarcastically.

Before I can defend myself, Brendan walks through the front door and shouts, "Hey, I'm home. Javy's soccer practice was awesome. What's for dinner?"

I take the opportunity to pull my arm free and scoot past my parents and into my bedroom. I can hear Dad talking with Brendan.

"Great. We're having a special meal tonight. Your mother has made tacos."

Silence comes from the kitchen. I hate to say it, but I enjoy Brendan's diversion. I remove my shoes and sit at my desk. Grabbing 'Myrtle the pen' and my journal, I start to write.

* * *

Journal Entry – A 'River' Day

<u>LEAP</u>
Growth spurt ✓

Body development ✓✓

Start period   don't ask

Especially don't ask Mrs. Miller. I'm sure she'd have something to say about me doing the growing thing wrong. I'd be the cause of my period not starting.

<u>BE SELF-SUFFICIENT</u>
Steve's mom makes me think I'm already self-sufficient. I don't want to say anything positive about my mother but... I know how to iron and who cares if my clothes are wrinkled or if I didn't brush my hair. Messy buns are popular, right? It would be exhausting to have a mother like Mrs. Miller. Am I saying my mother is better? NO. Just saying I don't want to have one like Steve's.

<u>DATING AND PREFERENCE</u>
I did a good job of being a pretend girlfriend for Alan, I think. Nadine is still confused but she'll figure it out eventually. I don't actually want Steve to understand about Alan. Let him think Alan and I are an item. Is that mean?

Alan is NOT a boy toy. I don't care what my mother says. She's wrong but I'm not telling her anything!

FIND YOUR IDENTITY
According to Alan, I don't need to tell everything I know. And I didn't even spout science facts this time. What does that say about me?

HAVE THREE GOOD FRIENDS, BELONG
I'm even more sure that I can add Alan to my list of friends. Alright, I meant to say he could be added to Nadine to make it two friends. I'm still not sure about Steve. Is he a friend? And what about Billy? What's up with him?

FEEL SAFE
That's a laugh. I never feel safe at home. I did feel safe in Mrs. Thomas' car. Well, except on the drive back when I don't think she was totally awake.

Linn

Walker

Gurke

Chapter 11
Trick-or-Treat

IT'S DAY TWENTY-NINE OF our Fright Fest. Brendan and I are watching *Freddy vs. Jason.* Every October, Brendan and I binge horror movies. We hold our Fright Fest lottery during the last weekend in September. Each of us brings possible titles to the table. A few years ago, I wrote down the rules so they can't change. As the youngest child, I know how to protect myself.

—Each lottery requires thirty movies. Participants have equal picks. Last year's Dumbwaiter gets the first pick.

—All movies must be available to view for free.

—Movies are chosen in viewing order. Lottery participants will begin with light-hearted or funny movies. By pick number five, the fright-o-meter must go up. Each member will use their final four picks to name the most frightening movies.

—Any participant who can't name an appropriate movie in ten seconds becomes the Dumbwaiter. If all movies are named quickly, the Dumbwaiter is the person who suggested the oldest movie.

—The Dumbwaiter serves snacks and runs errands during all viewing times for the entire month.

"Get in one of those cars and drive over his ass," I yell from the kitchen. "The car's a deadly weapon."

"You gotta find a weapon that will kill these freaks for good," Brendan yells back. "They aren't really alive."

I step into the living room so I can hear better.

"Where's our snack, Dumbwaiter?"

Since I'm the Dumbwaiter this year, Brendan's enjoying his superior position. I step back into the kitchen. "Mini pizzas are almost done."

There's always flour, salt, yeast, and oil in our pantry and leftovers in the fridge. If we were at Nadine's house, there would be store-bought frozen pizza in the freezer. But my mother doesn't believe in store-bought anything. Still thinks she's living on a farm, miles from a shopping center. So, I'm learning to cook. Not succeeding, but I'm trying.

I carry the bite-size pizzas into the room. "Your order, sir."

"What the hell's that?" Brendan asks when he sees my creation.

"Hot dog, artichokes, and olives on a base of cabbage," I say as I place the plate on the coffee table.

Brendan takes one and bites. He spits it back out. "This is crap."

"I may be the Dumbwaiter, but you can't complain. You didn't cook."

"Why did you add this movie to our list? It makes all high school boys seem stupid," Brendan gripes.

"It was free and ranks high on horror." I point at the screen. "It's not difficult to make boys look like idiots.

Nobody cares when they get sliced. The girls don't come off any better."

"This bathroom scene's ridiculous. Everyone knows bad things happen in bathrooms. I mean..."

We both jump when our doorbell rings.

Brendan recovers first. "Get the door, Dumbwaiter."

I slide off the couch as the television shows a tub overflowing with bloody water. Brendan won't pause the action.

I reach the front door and jump backward when I see what's on the other side. *Holy crap! Is that a woman?* The person's wearing a dress and has a scarf covering its head—is there hair under there? Woman or not, 'shim' looks like a short Hulk. I mean—whatever sex, it's green. And angry! I'm getting a foot-tapping, eye-flashing, pissed-off vibe. But—

"Open the door, Cupcake," it snarls.

I unlock the door and shout over my shoulder, "Aunt Lily's here."

"Finally," Aunt Lily says. "What took so long? Were you afraid to open the door for... me?"

"I didn't recognize you. What happened... to... your face?" I cringe at my words.

"This?" Aunt Lily points to herself. "A little elective adjustment to make sure I'm at my best. I didn't need it. I always look great, but a girl can't let herself go. Now, can she? I bought this bruise concealer from Emerald Cache. I can order you some. It reduces redness and covers up pimples."

She's insulting me? When she's the Hulk? "No thanks. I have lotion with SPF to keep my skin looking good."

"I need to buy it for your next birthday."

"Need? According to Dad, I don't *need* anything from Emerald Cache. You might want to buy it for me but that's a different matter."

I can hear Dad's words coming from my mouth. I'm just angry because she is using the word 'need' purposely. What I want to say is, you can kiss my—

Brendan walks into the foyer. "Aunt Lily? Oh, damn! That's... fugly... I mean, hello."

"Hello to you too, Sweetie." Aunt Lily sneers. "Now, put those muscles to work and help me with my bags. I assume I'll be staying in your room again."

"Uh, no." Brendan glances at me. He continues as I lean against the wall, "Grandma Rose is arriving on Saturday. She'll be using my room. Didn't Mom and Dad tell you?"

"No, they didn't. But I didn't exactly say I was coming." Aunt Lily attempts a smile, but her Hulk face isn't working. "This is an unexpected visit. I said I was going to help with the baby, but I had to leave and now I'm back."

Had to leave? Mom kicked you out. And your own mother didn't tell you she's visiting us? What's wrong with this family? Brendan's frozen in place. I walk between them. "Come with me. I'll get you settled in my room. Grandma Rose is going to rearrange Brendan's bedroom so the baby can fit in. Brendan's going to college soon, they can share the space."

"Don't go to any trouble, Cupcake. I don't want to be a problem."

Right, like I believe that! "No problem. Brendan and I can sleep on the couches."

Aunt Lily hoists her oversized purse onto her shoulder and begins to walk toward my room. "Tell your parents I'm here and bring my bags." She looks back at us. "Do you want me to make dinner tonight? I can be helpful."

"No!" Brendan and I answer in unison. I shake my head at the memory of Aunt Lily's over-peppered dinner.

"We're going out for dinner." Brendan glances at Aunt Lily. "You'll want to stay here."

"Why would I do that?" Aunt Lily asks.

"No reason... we're... umm... it's only dinner... you don't want to be out... in a public place. Right?"

I hate it when I enjoy watching Brendan struggle, but this is HI-larious.

"Why not?" Aunt Lily asks. "I love restaurants. Are you embarrassed by me, Sugar?"

"Of course not." Brendan turns around. "I'll go tell Mom and Dad you're here."

So they can escape? Or so you can?

"Of course." Aunt Lily turns back toward my room. "I'll freshen up."

I'm about to follow Brendan when I hear Aunt Lily. "My bags, Linn. Bring my bags."

I roll my eyes and grab some pink luggage. *This color should not be anywhere near Aunt Lily's greenness. You can call puke 'emerald' but it still looks like puke.*

"Don't worry about making the bed," I say. "We'll throw those sheets in the laundry. They should be ready by the time dinner's over."

Lily plops her largest suitcase on my bed before I can strip the sheets. "Where are we going for dinner? I need to decide what to wear."

"Diablo's Woodfire Grill. It's laid back. I'm going to wear my purple shirt with these jeans." I go to my closet and collect my shirt before Aunt Lily can block my access.

"Where I'm from, we dress elegantly. We're near a major city and track fashion trends."

"Which city? We're close to San Francisco and I haven't noticed a focus on fashion."

"Denver, obviously. The San Francisco hippies keep this place from having a fashion industry."

I immediately feel defensive. "That's a stereotype. San Francisco is a diverse city."

"It's so cute your parents have raised you to think people care about your opinion." Aunt Lily steps in front of my mirror and holds up a cardigan.

"It's in the sixties outside," I say. "A sweater will be too heavy. But, that's only my opinion." *I'm being spiteful, and I don't care.*

Aunt Lily smirks as if I'm a bug that needs squashing. "Okay, but I have to be trendy." She digs through her suitcase and removes an orange-striped blazer with three-quarter-length sleeves. "This will be perfect with my off-white shell and linen pants See? Elegant."

I can't think of anything positive to say. The contrast of the orange jacket next to her green-tinged face makes me want to crown her 'Queen of the Fright Fest.' Instead, I pull my journal out of the desk drawer. It's not safe in this room. I turn to walk out and nearly run over Dad. He apologizes and moves out of my way. I decide to stay in the laundry area and listen.

Dad continues into my room. "Lily, we're so glad you decided to—Jesus, Mary, and Joseph! What happened to you?"

Is it wrong to enjoy Dad's reaction? I snicker and join Brendan in the living room. "Are we going to watch the rest of the movie?"

"Aunt Lily's provided enough horror for one day, don't you think?"

Before I can answer, Dad hurries past. Brendan and I sit quietly, hoping to hear our parents' conversation. Dad's voice is too fast for our ears. Finally, Mom reacts. "No, no, no. This isn't happening to me. Not after last time."

Their discussion continues. When the bedroom door closes we can't make out what's being said. Finally, Dad walks back into the living room. "Brendan. Call the grill and place a takeout order. Then go pick it up." Dad pulls cash out of his wallet.

Brendan opens his eyes as wide as possible. "Aren't we going out for dinner? Or at least use Uber Eats?"

"No. Your mother's not feeling well. Don't be so lazy, takeout will be fine." Dad turns back to the bedroom.

I look at Brendan. "Opening your eyes wider doesn't make you look innocent."

"Shut it, Linn."

"Can I go with you to get the food?"

Brendan sighs. "If you call in the order."

An hour later Brendan and I return. We have ribs, street corn, roasted broccoli, and Diablo's famous charred salad. I start setting the table as Brendan unloads the food.

"Where is everyone?" I whisper.

"I'll go check on Mom and Dad." Brendan walks out of the room.

I grab a couple of platters from the kitchen and head back to the dining area. As I turn the corner, I nearly drop both dishes. "Aunt Lily! Your scarf... You've colored your hair. It's so... red."

"This?" Aunt Lily asks as she crimps her curls. "It's my natural color. The beautician reset the color back to normal."

I resist making a snarky comment and focus on her clothes. "Nice sweats. Did you travel to Denver to buy those?"

"No, Sweetie." Aunt Lily runs her hands down her hips. "These are my yoga pants. I picked them up at the studio in Cheyenne. I figure any clothes will do for dinner in this house."

I'm about to respond to Aunt Lily's tone but stop when I hear Brendan's voice before he enters the room. "Mom and Dad are coming. I told them... shhh-it. I mean... Lily... Hope you like the food we picked up. Why don't you take the corner chair?"

Brendan tilts his head toward the other end of the table. "Linn always sits on a left-hand corner. She's a lefty, ya know."

I realize what Brendan *isn't* saying—sit in a chair away from Aunt Lily. I snag the corner diagonally away from her. Brendan sits next to me at the head of the table. We continue to unload the food from our sitting positions.

As Mom and Dad enter the room, I study their faces. Mom's lip is already curled and tightens even more when she sees Aunt Lily. She must recognize our seating plan because she picks the chair across from me. That puts her next to her sister, but she won't have to look directly at her emerald complexion.

Dad pauses on his way toward the kitchen. "I'll pour drinks. What does everyone want?"

The word 'water' echoes around the table with varying levels of enthusiasm.

Aunt Lily's the only exception. "I need an adult beverage. Do you still have bourbon?"

"No," Dad answers. "Bella and I have decided to watch what we're drinking. You know, for the baby's sake. I can pour you a glass of wine if you like."

I look up at Dad. *Did he say they were cutting down on bourbon? Since when?*

"That'll have to do," Aunt Lily mumbles.

"Okay, one wine and water all around," Dad announces.

We begin serving and passing food around the table until only Dad's plate is empty.

"Here we go," Dad says as he delivers the drinks. He hands Aunt Lily a wine glass with a small amount of liquid in it. "I thought we had more but this is all that's left."

I study my plate so I won't give away my thoughts. *Breaking news: wine is missing in Bella's house... duh!*

Dad's been talking and not paying attention. He pauses in confusion as he delivers glasses to our unusual seats. Finally, he settles in the chair at the other end of the table. There's no way for Dad to avoid looking at Aunt Lily's bruised face. He glances at Brendan and me briefly and shakes his head.

"Lily," Dad says while filling his plate with food. "Who did your facelift?"

"It was a small procedure, George. Not a full facelift." Aunt Lily shakes her head. "And of course, I went to the best surgeon in Denver. He was perfect."

"No." Dad leans forward and studies Aunt Lily. "Your skin's so tight it's pulling your eyelids back and your hairline's different. They must have anchored the skin above your forehead and—"

"Get away from me, George," Aunt Lily hisses as she slides her chair out and stands. "I'm going to eat in my room."

Dad sits back and wrinkles his forehead. "I didn't mean anything, Lily. With all due respect, I was just telling you the truth."

Hulk-Lily attempts to roll her eyes but the muscles in her face aren't working. "Sorry, George, but I don't believe you know the truth." She turns and walks from the room, throwing a series of commands back at me. "Linn, you haven't changed the sheets yet. Get that done, and then collect my dinner dishes. I need to get my beauty rest, so don't dawdle."

I look around, preparing to complain when I notice Mom's lip is uncurled. Dad's observations usually upset her but not tonight. I scoop up a forkful of charred salad.

After dinner, I start Aunt Lily's chores. Grabbing some clean sheets from the laundry room and sighing before knocking on my own door.

Her Greenness opens the door with an empty plate in her hand. "It's about time." Aunt Lily holds the plate out to me. "The food was better than I expected."

I match Aunt Lily's stance and hold out the sheets. "Here are your sheets. Wanna trade?"

"I thought you were going to change the sheets," Aunt

Lily whines.

"Sure," I reply in my most innocent voice. "I'd be glad to change the sheets if you want to deliver your dish to the kitchen."

"No. Just give me those." Lily puts the plate on my desk and grabs the sheets.

I reach in and collect the dish. "Have a good night."

The sound of my door slamming barely covers Aunt Lily's growling through a list of complaints probably directed at me.

Brendan is still awake and watching Halloween movies in the family room. I walk past him, grab a blanket from the hall closet, and a book from the shelf. Moving into the front room, I stretch out on the couch and click on a lamp. "Maybe this visit will be shorter than the last one," I tell myself.

* * *

"Holy shit! Run!"

I sit up when I hear a male voice shouting outside our house. I glance at my phone. It's a few minutes after midnight. Thinking of the psychos in today's movie, I tiptoe to the window that runs along the side of the front door and peek out. Suddenly, Emma's staring back at me. I try to stifle the scream, but I'm loud enough to bring Brendan running from the family room.

"What the hell's going on?" he asks.

I slow my breathing and point at Emma on the other side of the window.

She knocks softly. "Linn, I need help."

I open the door. Brendan and I step onto the front porch. "Emma, what's going on?"

"I'm sorry." Emma chokes with tears in her voice. "Steve and I... we... were chalking your window. You know... like writing with the stuff they use to advertise cars. Steve

162

screamed and said to run. We didn't mean anything. It was a joke, a Halloween prank."

"Okay? I'm confused, why do you need help?"

"Linn," Brendan calls as he steps off the porch and crouches next to a person lying in the driveway. "Get Dad. It's Steve. He's awake but moaning."

I turn and hurry back into the house when Dad appears in the foyer.

Dad looks me up and down. "Why did you scream?"

"Steve's in the driveway and needs help."

"Who's Steve?"

"Steve Miller. He's in my grade at school and lives a couple of blocks over. I don't know what happened, please come." I lead the way.

Dad kneels next to Brendan in the driveway and begins to check on Steve. I look around to see what Emma's talking about. There are lines of neon orange chalk on my bedroom window like they were going to spell something. I jump when the curtains pull back to show Aunt Lily's green face.

I turn back to Emma. "I think I know what scared Steve. Did you see anything?"

"No, I was kneeling, getting another color of chalk. But I felt him run into me. He knocked me down. I got up, Steve stayed down. He was mumbling and holding his head."

"Linn," Dad interrupts. "Go get an ice bag. Brendan and I are going to move Steve into the house. He has a lump on his head. He might have a concussion. He's dazed but able to answer some basic questions. I'm going to call his parents and see if they want us to take him to a hospital."

Steve's lying on a couch inside my house with an ice bag on his head. Emma's pacing the length of the room. Dad's calling Steve's parents. This can't be good.

Without warning, Steve sits upright. "Monsters! Run!"

Emma hurries to his side. "It's okay," she says. "We're

in Linn's house. You fell and bumped your head but you're gonna be okay."

"How ya feeling, Bud?" Brendan asks.

"There... was... a... monster. The eyes were red, it had green skin, and I heard it speak in my head—said it was going to eat me like a cupcake." Steve squints up at Brendan and then scans the others in the room. "You believe me, don't you?"

"I believe you," I answer. "But it wasn't a monster. You saw my Aunt Lily. She's staying in my room and recently had... well... her face..."

"What's wrong?" Aunt Lily asks as she enters the room. "I can't sleep with this ruckus."

Steve pushes himself back on the couch cushions as far as possible. "Don't let it eat me, Linn. I'm too young to die."

I step between Steve and Aunt Lily. "It's okay, Steve. It's just my aunt. She had a facelift. Trust me, nobody wants to snack on you tonight."

"How many times do I have to tell you? It wasn't a full facelift!" Aunt Lily sits in Dad's favorite chair and pouts.

Dad walks back over to Steve and checks the ice bag. "Your father's on his way to pick you up. He thought you were asleep." Dad scowls at Emma. "Do I need to call your parents?"

"No, sir," Emma squeaks. "I'll ride with Steve."

"You should call the police instead."

We all turn toward the voice in the hallway. *Oh crap. It's Mom and the look on her face explains where the missing wine has gone. Can this night get any worse?*

Dad is the first to react. "Bella, let's not go overboard. They're children and no real harm was done."

"Children?" Mom snarls. "You mean juvenile delinquents, don't you?"

"I'm sure these two aren't a threat to anyone. Right?"

Dad waits for Steve to agree. Steve's frozen in place and unable to speak.

Emma's shaking her head up and down. "We were—having fun."

Mom steps farther into the room and points at Emma. "There are laws designed to protect us from the likes of you." She turns to Dad. "Tell them, George. You always have statistics and facts rattling around in your head. Try to use some of it to support me for once."

Dad kneels next to Steve and explains. "There's a midnight curfew. If you're out past then, you can be fined five hundred dollars."

Steve shakes his head. "But it's Halloween."

"No. Halloween is two nights from now," Dad says. "The city has passed laws. Anyone under eighteen can't be out past midnight. Even on Halloween."

Steve looks at me. "Linn, we were going to ask you to go out with our group on Halloween. Is he saying you can't go?"

I open my mouth to respond but Mom speaks first. "Linn? Going out with a bunch of criminals? Absolutely not! Linn will be here, handing out candy. And you two should be finding ways to pay your fine. George? Are you going to call the police or not?"

"Bella, I've already called Steve's father and I'm sure he'll deal with the kids." Dad stands and walks over to Mom. He continues to talk in a tone so low I only catch a few words—'injury' and 'lawsuit' stand out.

Mom's lip curls more as she considers Steve. "How's your head? Better? I hear you thought my sister was a monster." Mom nods toward Aunt Lily. "An understandable mistake."

"Hey!" Aunt Lily protests.

Mom continues in her scariest teacher voice. "We'll ignore you breaking curfew, trespassing, and vandalizing our property. However, if I catch you around here, I'll have you arrested. Now, grow up! I'm going back to bed and forgetting this ever happened."

"Me too," Aunt Lily says as she stands. "Linn, you'll need to clean the bedroom window tomorrow."

Before anyone else can speak, we hear a honk from our driveway.

"That's Dad," Steve says. He stands and wobbles.

Brendan grabs Steve to keep him upright. "I'll help you out to the car."

"No. Please don't," Steve says. "Dad won't want anyone to see him this late at night."

"Steve Miller? Is your father Mike Miller of Miller's Autoplex? Did you take these from your father's business?" Dad holds the neon window chalk out to Steve.

"Yeah, Dad sells cars. This stuff's all over the house. I didn't think he'd miss it." Steve grabs the markers and pockets them. "Come on Emma, we gotta go. My dad's gonna be pissed."

Dad locks the front door behind Steve and Emma. He turns and frowns at us. "Damn it! Steve's father is a member of the school board. The school board is my boss. Steve's prank could cause me problems at work."

Brendan and I look at each other. Dad doesn't swear much. Neither of us says anything.

Dad shakes his head and leaves the room, mumbling.

* * *

Journal Entry – Removing the Halloween Mask

I'm not allowed to go out for Halloween. Big surprise! I haven't been allowed to trick-or-treat since I was ten. My parents said costumes were childish and I wasn't a child.

But I'm not an adult either. So what does it

mean to have a childhood? Is it being free to play? Or not having to pay bills? Alan's right, we don't pay bills, but our free labor saves the family money. Shouldn't childhood be an opportunity to start growing up?

LEAP AND PARENTS

I've been wondering if Mom and Dad have finished growing up.

Okay, LEAP 1-3 are physical developments that happen naturally as you get older. And yes, Mom and Dad know their preference, but no longer need to date (5).

Still, the rest of the list doesn't describe my parents.

(4 Self-sufficient) Mom can't drive worth crap and Dad has to control the alcohol. Doesn't "self" mean taking care of me, myself, and I?

(6 Find your identity) Besides being TEACHERS. Mom pretends she's perfect. Dad lies about Mom but tells the truth about others? What's that?

(7 Have three good friends) If you ask me they only have each other. There are people they invite to parties—not enough!

(8 Feel safe) Can Mom and Dad feel safe if they are always lying? Maybe they should take off the Halloween mask they wear all year.

How can they tell me, Steve, or anyone else to

grow up? I say, "You first."

I'm being spiteful again. Mom isn't always bad. She makes fantastic cookies when she wants to. She used to sew clothes. She used to pretend to be caring by doing all the mother stuff everyone expects. That was in the past. Now, she's unhappy about being a mother. Then she drinks and makes everyone miserable. Still, I wouldn't want Aunt Lily to be my mother.

Note to self: ask Grandma why her kids are so messed up.

Linn

Walker

Gurke

Chapter 12
Oops

I'VE LEARNED MY LESSON! I thought both September and October would be good, they weren't. So, let's just admit it. November is crap, my life is crap. Even if my relatives weren't here, I'd say November is already bad. It's a pattern, a bad luck spiral.

I sit in the front room and lean forward to stretch my muscles before attempting to sleep. Aunt Lily's been in my room for five days. I feel a lumpy-couch-sleeping spasm in my back. I hold my breath when a shadow moves toward my bed/couch.

Brendan plops down next to me. "Have you noticed?"

I let out a sigh of relief, it's just Brendan. "Noticed what?"

"Grandma arrived, Aunt Lily's still here, Mom's gonna pop, we're sleeping on couches, and it's the longest day of the year."

"I'm confused." I glance at the date on my watch. "The longest day of the year is the summer solstice and that was in June."

"Summer soulstix?" Brendan's eyebrows pull down. "What are you talking about?"

"*Solstice.* When the sun is in the sky for the longest time. This year it was shining for over twelve hours. That makes it the longest day. Right?" *Why am I asking Brendan? He barely knows Earth's a planet.*

"Tell me this, Ms. Nerd—did summer soulstix have

more than twenty-four hours in it?"

"No…" I hesitate, knowing I've walked into a Brendan trap. "Does today?"

"Yes." Brendan smirks. "It's daylight saving tonight. At two in the morning, the clocks turn back one hour. That means we'll have a twenty-five-hour day. Exactly when Grandma, Aunt Lily, and Mom are all together."

"Grandma isn't bad. I'm glad she's here. And technically, tomorrow will be the longest day. That's the day after Grandma Rose arrived." *I should give Brendan credit for catching me, but I'm more interested in not being wrong.*

"Big difference." Brendan shakes his head. "Today, tomorrow, doesn't matter. Evil shit's focused on this house for an extra hour. Mom having a baby is nasty enough, and Grandma isn't bad—by herself. But there's something else. Whatever it is, it's coming for you, Barbara."

"I've seen *Night of the Living Dead* too," I reply. "Are you about to die? In that movie, right after teasing Barbara, the brother dies. I love that scene."

Brendan lowers his voice. "I'm getting some bad vibes in this house."

"I know, but what can we do to help?"

"You can't do anything, Idjit. Shit happens and this family has stepped into a steaming pile. Believe me, things are about to get messy."

"Things are already messy," I respond. "What do you think's going to go wrong?"

"Grandma Rose, Aunt Lily, and Mom together? With all these wackos in the same house, what could possibly go right?" Brendan stands to leave the room. When he reaches the hallway, he looks back into the dark room. "Get some sleep, Spaz. You're gonna need it."

I press a finger to my twitching eye. "Thanks for nothing, Bro," I say to the empty room.

* * *

The next morning, I find Grandma in the kitchen. "Why're you awake so early?"

"Habit." Grandma smiles at me. "Living on a farm, I had to get up at the crack of dawn. I'd get breakfast going so your grandfather had energy for his work. Why are you up?"

"I couldn't sleep." I lean on the counter. "I'm on a couch. When the sun shines in, it wakes me up. I miss my blackout curtains."

Grandma pats the chair. "Sit down and I'll get you a slice of toast."

"You don't have to serve me, Grandma. I can take care of myself."

"I know, but grandmas use food to show love. A little love toast never hurt anyone."

"Thank you," I mumble as I lower myself into a seat. I wipe the tears forming in my eyes. *Why do I cry every time someone's nice to me?*

Grandma delivers two plates of toast and a couple of glasses of milk.

"You don't drink coffee?" I ask.

"I've never liked the taste and I don't need it to wake up. I lay down at night and sleep. When the sun comes up, I'm awake. I turned over this morning and thought of five positives."

Not this again! Grandma's letter from last year explained her positives and how she got 'Jed the cow' from positive thinking. She's never mentioned losing her cow. I've heard about it, just not in a positive way. I don't want a cow at my house, but I'm too tired to argue. "What's today's positives?"

Grandma raises a finger as she ticks off her thoughts. "First, I'm in California, with you. Second, Bella's going to have me another grandchild. Third, your parents do work that's a service to others. Fourth, you and your brother are getting an education. And finally, I'm still above ground so praise the Lord." Grandma throws her hands wide triumphantly. "Do you remember when I challenged you to think of positive truths?"

I lower my head and focus on the remaining toast. "Yes, Grandma, I've been writing about my truths in a journal." *I decide not to tell her about my lack of positives or not wanting a cow.*

"See? If you fill your brain with blessings, there's no room for darkness."

I can't help it. My brain immediately lists dark thoughts. Slut, lying, blame, scars, and alcohol. How can I ask my question without hurting Grandma?

"What was Mom like as a child?"

Grandma's smile disappears. "We lived on a farm. Your Grandpa Jed said everyone had to contribute. The girls had chores. They took care of the livestock and helped during potato season. He couldn't abide a person lying around doing nothing. Lily tried to have fun, but Bella took everything too seriously."

"What do you mean by too seriously?" I ask while chewing the last bite of my love toast.

"Deaths are normal on a farm." Grandma reaches over and strokes my hair. "Bella couldn't find any positives in how fragile life was."

"That explains a lot," I moan.

"A lot of what?" Grandma asks.

"Why both Mom and Aunt Lily are unhappy." I look at Grandma and regret my words. "Sorry, I didn't mean to say anything rude. It's... they are so... I don't know... sad."

Grandma leans back in her chair and lets out a sigh. "How much do you remember about your Grandpa Jed?"

"I don't remember Grandpa much. Except he said he liked my hair."

"By the time you came along he wasn't himself and

the cancer was in him. I wouldn't wish that death on anyone. In the end, he wanted to show you and Brendan how much he cared. He did love your hair." Grandma strokes my hair, again. "Before the cancer, Jed was a hard man. Don't get me wrong. I know he loved me—and the girls. But he expected too much of them. Jed's religious views weren't a good fit for daughters. He believed girls should be subservient. Every time Bella or Lily had an opinion, Jed said they were acting evil. When they started to develop into their womanhood, Jed saw sin everywhere. I have to believe he meant well, but my girls never felt important. I tried to show them love, but I was never enough for them." Grandma pulls a tissue out of her pocket and runs it across her eyes. "They wanted Jed to accept them. It's like he was the only parent they could see."

"I'm sorry. I didn't mean to make you sad."

"Sweetheart, you can't make me sad. I fill my soul with positives and blessings."

"You're enough Grandma for me," I whisper.

Grandma hugs me and whispers, "I love you." She pulls back and pats my hand. "Now, let's get down to business and do something productive today—for Bella."

"Sure, something nice." I fake a grin and ignore my spiteful feelings about Mom.

Grandma goes to the pantry and hands me a series of ingredients. We have yeast, salt, and sugar lined up when Brendan walks into the kitchen with a damp towel around his neck.

"I wish coffee didn't taste like burnt shit." He opens the fridge. "I need caffeine."

"There's a Coke hiding in the back," I offer.

Brendan turns to me. "I don't drink carbonated beverages. I'm an athlete. My body is my temp—" He stops short when Grandma steps out of the pantry.

"Good morning." Grandma smiles. "Every year you

look more like your Grandpa Jed."

Brendan frowns and blows air through his nose. He sounds like a bull getting ready to charge. "What're you two doing?"

"We're going to make bread," Grandma replies, "but we need more ingredients."

"I can go to the store with Brendan," I say excitedly.

Brendan mumbles, "I'll get dressed."

I dig a notepad and pen out of the junk drawer. "What should we buy?"

Grandma lists ingredients without needing a recipe.

Brendan walks back into the room with the car keys in his hand. He grabs my list and glances at it. "You want what?" Brendan stares at Grandma Rose.

I pull Brendan toward the door. "Let's go."

"Flour, at least a hundred-pound sack," Grandma Rose says without taking her eyes off the task of measuring sugar.

"I don't think stores sell flour in bags that large."

Grandma looks up incredulously. "Why not?"

"Nobody needs a hundred pounds of flour." Brendan's more confused than Grandma.

"City folk," Grandma grumbles. "Buy as much as you can. There's some in the pantry."

Brendan shakes his head and turns to leave.

Aunt Lily coming into the kitchen and demanding coffee hurries us out the door.

Once we're on our way Brendan asks, "How much bread does she plan to make?"

I feel the need to defend Grandma Rose. "She used to cook for farmhands. I remember the flour bags in her house. A hundred pounds is a small amount."

"But why now?"

"She's trying to keep us busy. So we don't think about Mom and the baby coming."

"People at the grocery store will think we've lost it. And I don't look like Grandpa Jed."

I almost laugh. "How will we even bake all the bread? We don't have that many pans."

Brendan parks and we enter the store. He grabs a cart, heads for the baking aisle, and points at the flour. Clearly, he's waiting for me to collect the bags. Why does it seem every bag of flour is leaking?

Brendan pushes our cart to a lane where he doesn't know anyone.

When we reach the car, I ask, "Why didn't you go to the line where Sue was bagging?"

"How do you explain this much flour?"

He starts the car and pulls out of the parking lot. "Has Grandma ever challenged you to think positive thoughts?" I ask.

"Why would Grandma want me to be positive?"

"Grandma says being positive improves your life. She wants me to think good thoughts." I consider what to say. "Maybe she wants you to be upbeat."

"Grandma lived on a fly-infested, manure-smelling farm. She needs to be positive. I'm already awesome." Brendan smirks. "I've told you this a million times."

"Silly me," I respond. "How could I forget?"

Brendan parks in front of the house.

He opens the back car door. "Grab some bags. It's going to take a few trips to get it all."

I take a deep breath and attempt to channel Grandma's positive thinking. "Living with you fills me with blessings."

"And I thought you had gas."

* * *

Brendan pulls into the school and parks. "No chauffeuring service today. Take the bus home."

I grab my stuff from the back seat before Brendan can

lock the car. "I'm taking Grandma's advice and focusing on the positives. So, I appreciate your help, Brendan."

"See ya later, Zits." Brendan throws me a wave and walks away.

When I arrive at the quad, Nadine and Alan are waiting. "Thanks for meeting me."

"What's up?" Nadine asks. "Your message had me concerned."

"I'm fine, really."

Alan looks at the items in my hands. "You said 'gifts in the quad.' What ya got?"

"Bread. Brendan and I spent all day cooking with Grandma Rose. Grandma used every pan Mom owns. Our house's overrun with loaves, rolls, Hungarian coffee cakes, and fried bread. I brought a small loaf for each of you." I hand them each a wrapped packet.

Nadine attempts to smell through the wrap. "Thanks, Linn. I love the homemade bread that comes out of your house." She pauses. "Are you sure... I mean..."

"Don't worry," I laugh. "I'm positive there's no soap in the bread."

Nadine leans forward. "Is it okay you brought this? Your mom won't get upset?"

"Nope. We made so many, nobody will notice a few missing loaves. Besides, with Grandma's arrival, the house is almost normal. Mom's on maternity leave and spends all her time in bed. Dad went outside to do yard work. It was a good weekend."

Nadine shrugs. "Well, that explains why you seem happy."

"Grandma challenged me to think positive thoughts. I'm determined to find one positive thing during each class."

"Let me know how that goes. I'm going to save my positive bread for later. Thanks again." Nadine picks up her backpack and heads toward her locker.

I turn to see what Alan has to say. He looks like a chipmunk collecting nuts and half of his loaf is missing. "I thought you'd eat that at lunch."

Alan talks around the bread in his mouth. "Whaf ate?"

"What?"

He holds up a finger and swallows the wad in his mouth. "Why wait? This is too good to save. Besides, you've brought more." He eyes the bag in my other hand.

"Those are for Ms. Hess and Ms. Garcia."

"I thought we didn't like them. You said—"

"I know what I said. That was..." I stop to think. "Two months ago. They aren't bad."

Alan crosses his eyes. "Whatever." He stands to leave and takes another huge bite of bread. "Thafs agimm."

"You know that loaf took four hours to make. So, you're welcome." I call to his retreating back. Sometimes it's difficult to be positive.

After English class, I find Nadine waiting for me outside the locker room. We fall into our synchronized walk. "Got any good thoughts to share?"

"Yep. I'm doing great." We take a towel from Mrs. Portia and walk into the changing room. "In band, I decided I like being a terrible clarinet player."

"How's that a positive?" Nadine asks.

"If you're good, you have to sit in the front row. I'm bad and that puts me on the back row near the trumpets. The back row's a lot more fun."

"Okay, I guess that's a plus. What else have you got?"

"I got an A on my math test."

"You always get A's in math," Nadine says. "How does that make today different?"

"When Mr. Teague passed out the tests, I didn't cover my score. I'm tired of hiding my papers in case someone else feels bad."

"That's absolutely a positive." Nadine steps up on the changing bench and proclaims, "Linn's a math whiz—she's out and she's proud."

I pull Nadine back down. "Stop," I laugh.

"And in English? Was it positive?"

"Ms. Hess's class is always positive. We developed evidence-based arguments. It's not the same as arguing. It's about developing a reason for your statements. I'm a positive, honest, evidence-based rock star. And I gave Ms. Hess some homemade bread. She's happy."

"So, little Miss Rock Star, what do you think will be positive about P.E. today?"

I glance in the locker room mirror. "Sweating is a great way to treat mountain-sized zits. And I'm going to keep my shirt on today."

Nadine looks at me from under her lashes. "It's not that noticeable. Besides, it's probably a stress zit. Either way, a workout will help. Maybe I'll take my shirt off today."

"As if." We both laugh.

At lunch, I give my last loaf of bread to Ms. Garcia and share some rolls with Steve. He's so busy eating, he doesn't have time to drive me crazy. *Note to self—feed the Dorknut.*

"That was great bread," Steve says as we walk toward science. "Did you help make it?"

I stop my eyes from rolling. I know where this is going. "Mostly it was Grandma." I can't help the fact that Steve and I have science together, or our last names. But, I can try to control my eye rolls.

I sit in my alphabetically assigned seat. If only someone had a last name starting with H-L, they would be between Steve and me. I'm not that lucky.

Ms. Baker begins to speak, and Steve's foot starts tapping, again. I grit my teeth and think positive thoughts. *Steve can't help it. He's hyper and I'm not—that's a blessing.*

I can handle this. It's only fifty minutes out of my day. Ignore it. World Geography is next... Without thinking I turn in my seat. "If you don't stop tapping, I'm going to beat the junk out of you!"

Steve freezes. He's trying to hold still. "Sorry," he whispers.

I feel bad. Steve still has a bruise from the chalk incident. "Oh crap, go ahead and move. But put your feet on the floor." So much for Grandma's challenge. Fault-line Linn couldn't rock the positives for an entire school day.

I turn back to find the teacher frowning at me. "Ms. Gurke. In this classroom, we address others with respect. Threats of violence aren't allowed..." She glances at the classroom door to see who is knocking then turns back to me. "As I was saying, we do not..." The knocking gets louder. Ms. Baker throws up her hands, stomps to the door, and jerks it open. "What?"

"Sorry to interrupt. I need Linn." Brendan hands Ms. Baker a note and looks around the room for me. "Linn, we gotta go."

I push everything I can into my backpack. I don't know why Brendan is here, but I'm not going to question any excuse to leave.

Ms. Baker points a finger at me. "We'll finish this discussion later, young lady."

"Yes, ma'am," I say as I hurry into the hallway.

Brendan looks at me for a moment and heads toward the exit. "What was *that* about?"

"I don't know," I lie. "Why are you here? What's going on?"

"It's Mom." Brendan pulls the car keys out. "Dad called the school. They're at the hospital having the baby. He wants us to come as soon as possible."

"It's not time yet." I'm practically running to keep up. "Mom's not due until November 20th. That's almost two weeks from now."

"Clearly, Oops doesn't care about your schedule."

"Is there something wrong? I mean is he... is Mom..."

Brendan hits the unlock button. "Do I look like someone who knows about having babies? Get in, Spaz."

I try to be positive during our drive to the hospital, but Grandma's good thoughts have left me. "Brendan, stop. That's a red—"

"Fuck the lights. It's an emergency."

I brace myself as Brendan takes each turn too fast. The navigation app isn't showing any police in the area but that doesn't mean—

"Watch the truck!"

"I've got this. Now shut it."

I press my lips together and study the side-view mirror. Maybe if I focus on the road behind us I won't be so scared. There are no disasters on the road we've already traveled. Is that the best way to approach this whole situation? Put the fear in front of you away and think positive thoughts. After all, I haven't yet died in a fiery crash and the baby is fine. Maybe.

Once the car pulls into the visitor's lot, I chance a comment. "Congratulations, you set a new land-speed record for driving on side streets."

Brendan glances at me. "Stop yapping and keep up."

I hurry after Brendan and follow him through the hospital's revolving door. Dad is waiting for us in the lobby, wearing his work suit and a loosened tie.

"Brendan, Linn, so glad you're here."

"Where's Mom? Is everything okay? When do you think the baby will arrive? Is Aunt Lily here?" I look around the lobby. "What about Grandma?"

Dad laughs. "Give me a chance to speak, Linn. Come sit over here and I'll explain." He directs us to a group of chairs in the front lobby.

Brendan and I sit, lean forward, and wait for Dad to continue.

"Eric's here. I counted, and he has all the expected fingers and toes. They're doing the normal tests on Eric." Dad smiles. "It all happened fast—about five hours. Your mom's in recovery and the doctor's monitoring her. Soon they'll assign her a room. Then you can see her."

Brendan nods. "What do you need us to do?"

"Once you see your mom and Eric, go home. Tell Rose and Lily what's going on."

"They didn't come with you?" I ask. *If Aunt Lily is anywhere near, I need to be ready.*

Dad shakes his head. "No, your mother didn't want them here. She told them it was most likely false labor."

"Do they know the baby's here?" Brendan asks.

"Yes, I called them after I called your school. They're not happy, particularly Lily." Dad sighs. "Sorry, but I have to throw you two under this bus. I'm going to stay here tonight with your mother. Linn, when you get home can you grab a change of clothes for both of us? We didn't get around to packing a bag."

"Sure, I can do that."

"Brendan." Dad reaches for his wallet and passes over some cash. "Help your Grandmother with dinner or pick up something. When you can, bring the clothes back. If you can both get here that would be great. But don't bring Rose and Lily. I'll deal with them tomorrow. I haven't contacted my family either."

Dad's phone buzzes. He looks down. "She has a room. Let's go see her."

Brendan and I stand and follow Dad to the elevator.

When we enter Mom's room, a woman in light blue scrubs is standing at a rolling computer cart. She turns to greet us. "Ah, these must be the other Gurke children. I'm Doctor Johnson." She gives Brendan and me each a light handshake and then squirts sanitizer into her palms. "Your mother did a great job. She's a trooper, never complained once."

Dad walks past the doctor to the other side of Mom's bed and takes her hand. She doesn't have the energy to respond.

I consider the hand-sanitized doctor and feel distrust. "Why are Mom's arms so skinny?"

"She did just have a baby. It takes a lot out of a person."

"But they're skinnier than before she got pregnant. And she's not speaking."

"She'll be fine. She has you two as helpers, right?" Doctor Johnson looks at Brendan for an answer, but he's not engaging with anyone.

I step forward so the doctor can't ignore me. "Where's the baby?"

"Eric's in the nursery until they complete the tests." Doctor Johnson's smile is slipping.

"What kinds of tests have you done?" I search my brain for the words I learned from the websites. "What's his APGAR score? Have you checked for any..." I check to see if Mom's listening, but she has a faraway look, "... syndromes?"

Doctor Johnson frowns. "Your brother was born early. He's eighteen inches long and weighs six pounds, four ounces. He's not considered premature. His APGAR score's normal. The APGAR is a quick test and not indicative of future issues." She puts her hands on her hips. "This is why I tell my patient's families not to rely on the internet for their information."

"Then why do you still perform the test?" I argue.

"Because it gives us... never mind." Doctor Johnson turns to Dad. "Mr. Gurke, can I have a moment of your time? In the hallway?"

Dad reluctantly puts Mom's hand down and follows

the doctor out of the room. I take his place by Mom's bed, but I don't reach for her hand. *It wouldn't feel natural.* I try to remember when I felt comfortable touching my mother—nope, nothing. If I don't care about Mom, then why am I arguing with the doctor? Do I care about Eric? Yes.

Brendan murmurs to me. "Is that your version of positive thinking?"

"No, I've given up on positives. Science stuff pops into my head and runs out of my mouth. I can't control it. The doctor dismissed me. Just because I'm young, doesn't mean I'm stupid." I exhale slowly. "What about you? Since when did you stop talking?"

Brendan glances at Mom and then turns to me. "And talk about my mother having a baby? This is why I have a sister. It's your job to know all the girl-parts stuff."

"Sorry to disappoint you but, I don't know much about having a baby."

"Then where did you get all those questions? I've never even heard of an appgate test."

"APGAR." I look down at Mom's hand but I still can't bring myself to pick it up. "The doctor was right. I did a few internet searches at school. I mean, who doesn't?"

"Me. Obviously."

* * *

"Well, there you have it." Brendan gestures at Eric behind the viewing glass.

"Have what?" I ask while watching the baby and his incubator.

Brendan glances at me. "Our future, Spaz."

"They're treating him for jaundice. How's this our future?"

Brendan gestures toward the glass. "They tell us Oops needs light for his liver. Instead, he's lying around in his bikini diaper, wearing shades, and napping. It's like he's at the beach."

"You heard the nurse. It's called phototherapy."

Brendan wags his finger. "He's getting a tan. This kid has it figured. Milking this jaundice thing while we do all the work. Slacker!"

"You're going to college next year, so you're saying I'll be doing all the work."

"Sucks to be you. Let's go home and deal with the rela-freaks."

As Brendan drives, I send messages to my friends so they don't worry.

> ME: left school early - baby here - everyone in hospital but good

> NADINE: Thanks! I was worried. Steve said Brendan checked you out. Need help?

> ME: not yet - will let you know

> ALAN: U left?

I shake my head in disbelief and slide my phone into a pocket.

* * *

Journal Entry — November Plus and Minus List

Mom came home first. Her arms are too skinny. We all tiptoe around and hope Mom will bounce back. Well, everyone except Aunt Lily. She's only interested in herself.

When Eric finally came home, I tried to check

for fetal alcohol syndrome. Obviously, there was a liver issue but he's doing better. I don't see any deformities but I don't know how babies should develop. The internet says these kids might have small eyes, a small head, an upturned nose, or a smooth upper lip. There aren't any pictures of this. What are babies supposed to look like? His eyes aren't small but they also aren't large either. What does that mean? Eric definitely doesn't have the small head thing. In fact, I think his head's fat. I should say "large" but I'm not nice and his head's fat.

Now I'm sure I'm not like Mom. I'll never be like her. I think Eric's kinda cute. With the yellow color going away, he's turning kinda pink. Even if he was completely ugly, I know I would never hurt him. The first time I held him I knew. No bottle is as important as Eric.

Only problem is he cries ALL THE TIME! That could be a syndrome issue, but I don't know. I mean, how are you supposed to check balance, memory, or changing moods when all they do is eat, cry, and poop? The crying could be about Eric's mood but it's not changing. His mood's more like consistently bad. The websites say "problems may develop." I want to know when, where, and why. Dad says I want answers before the questions have been asked. Science and logic should give me answers—just saying!

Mom tried to breastfeed once or twice and gave

up. Maybe he's smarter and understands she can't be trusted. He'll drink from a bottle—oh crap. I just realized what I wrote. This kid likes bottles. Guess he takes after Mom.

<u>LEAP</u>
LEAP 8, Feeling safe is my biggest issue.

I feel safer when Grandma and her love toast are here. I still don't feel safe with Mom, but I know I can survive her nastiness. Most people would count being spiteful and not caring as a negative. I say it's my superpower. Those skills help me survive.

Besides Grandma, I feel somewhat safe with Brendan. He cares about me, I think. Brendan says he's awesome and pretends he feels confident, but I've seen his scars. I'm worried about Brendan. Now Eric has been added to my list of things that aren't safe. Poor thing doesn't know the problems he faces. There's untrustworthy rela-freaks, a drunk-ass mother, a father in denial, and two scarred siblings. Maybe babies can sense bad vibes and that's why he cries all the time.

Linn

Walker

Gurke

Chapter 13
Shaken

DAY THREE OF ERIC at home and he's finally asleep. He likes me to walk him around and sing. *Why? I have a terrible voice. And memory—what comes after the diamond ring turns to brass?*

I'm humming "Hush Little Baby," as I enter the living room and sit next to Grandma. "Grandma, can we cook a special meal?"

* * *

"Ta-Da! Chicken and dumplings by Grandma Rose and me." I place the steaming dish on a hot pad in the middle of the table. "Side salads are build-your-own."

Brendan reaches for the hot dish. "Let's eat before Eric wakes up and starts crying."

"Brendan, wait." Grandma Rose holds out her hands. "I'd like to give the blessing tonight." She's been here for two weeks, and we all know what she expects. Brendan reaches for my hand. Everyone bows their head while Grandma prays. "Thank you, Lord, for providing such a bounty. Thank you for the continued recovery of Bella and Eric. Thank you to Linn, for making this special day into a party. Amen."

"I don't know what's so special about today," Aunt Lily mumbles.

"It's special because Bella and Eric are home," Dad says.

"Special occasion or not," Brendan says as he slurps up a dumpling, "this tastes great."

"Glad you like it," Grandma responds. "This meal will cure what ails you."

"It's a little carb-heavy," Mom says, pushing a spoon through her dinner. "Good thing I've lost my baby fat."

Aunt Lily points a finger at Mom. "Lost your baby fat? In less than two weeks? Not possible."

I check to see what Dad will say but he remains quiet. *Something's wrong.*

Mom curls her lip. "Self-control, Lily. Decide to lose weight and watch what you eat."

"Maybe you can self-control those saggy boobs back into place," Aunt Lily grumbles.

Dad keeps his head down and speaks between bites of food. "Bella's doing great and she's back to her pre-baby weight."

"When's your next check-up?" Brendan asks Mom. "Ask your doctor about weight loss. You're too skinny."

"I'm fine," Mom replies. "I'm better than fine."

I attempt to defend all women. "Mom's suppressed appetite and weight loss are signs of postpartum depression. It's not unusual—I looked on the internet."

The sound of Mom's chair scraping draws my attention. She's standing with her 'teacher finger' pointing at me. "I do *not* have postpartum depression," she hisses. "I've never had mental problems."

"M-Mom," I stammer. "Postpartum depression isn't a mental issue. It's caused by—"

"Stop," Mom yells. "Don't insult me in my own house. I'm fine. I'm better than anyone else at this table. Especially you, Linn." Mom begins to leave but turns to throw another insult my way. "You don't deserve a mother."

I pull my mouth closed. It takes effort to act normal. Grandma seems to be holding back tears. Brendan's as still as possible.

Dad stands to follow Mom. He leans down and whispers, "She doesn't have postpartum depression. She can't have any problems." He turns and leaves the room.

"I admit I had postpartum depression," Aunt Lily says. "Three times and not one baby to show for it. It's not fair." Aunt Lily puts her spoon down and considers Grandma Rose. "Bella gets everything—three living children and no postpartum depression. I get all the bad stuff. How is that fair?"

Grandma looks at Aunt Lily. "This isn't a competition, Lily. In life, there's no rhyme or reason. Focus on your blessings. There are so many."

"That's crap, and you know it." Aunt Lily stands and turns her back on Grandma Rose. "Don't forget to clean up this mess, Linn."

"I'll help with the dishes." Grandma Rose pushes her chair out.

"No, Linn and I can handle this," Brendan says. "You go rest or watch a show." Brendan leans forward. "I hate to say it, but I was right."

"Did you cause Fault-line Linn to open her mouth? Did you say I'm unlovable?"

"Don't listen to her. You're lovable... maybe," Brendan whispers. "I predicted something bad was coming. *Night of the Living Dead*? I said it was coming for you, Barbara. How many times do I have to tell you? The way to survive this family is to shut the fuck up. You can think anything you want, but don't say it out loud." Brendan stands up. "Come on, let's get these dishes done."

* * *

Nadine hands her unused towel to Mrs. Portia as we leave P.E. "Why do we have to learn B-ball? Nobody likes this game except Javy. And he's good at everything."

I turn away so Nadine doesn't see me blush. "Don't you just hate him? Glad it's lunchtime. I brought leftovers. Grandma's bread makes everything taste good."

"What?" Nadine teases. "The best thing isn't my sparkling personality?"

"I forgot. Your sparkle is first and then Grandma's bread." I relax into a cafeteria chair.

"That looks good," Steve says as I finish my lunch.

I lick my fingers. "It was. Sorry, I didn't bring extra."

"Maybe next time." Steve smiles.

This guy doesn't get sarcasm.

"Gotta go," I say, "don't want any trouble with Ms. Baker."

Steve follows me into the hallway. "I told Ms. Baker I wasn't upset when you yelled at me. I don't think you'll actually hit me. I'm too loveable."

I roll my eyes. I refuse to discuss Steve's lovability or lack thereof. "Ms. Baker's been cool about my outburst. She heard the baby was born and said I must've felt stressed."

Steve continues, "I've really been trying not to tap my foot on your chair."

"Good. 'Cause I don't want to hurt you."

Steve laughs as we take our seats in the classroom. "Funny, Linn." He leans forward. "You're joking, right?"

I open my book to the pages listed on the board.

"Linn?"

A better person would answer him, but I'm in a spiteful mood. I focus on taking notes about biosphere factors. My desk begins to bounce. I can't stop myself. I turn on Steve. "I swear, I'm going to knock you..."

Steve's feet are nowhere near me. His desk and mine both take one more bounce and stop.

"Earthquake," Ms. Baker announces. "Everyone drop and cover."

Most of us slide to the ground and curl up under our

desks.

Ms. Baker stands at the front of the room. "Emma. Under your table, now."

"B-but," Emma stammers, "it's over."

"We've discussed this." Ms. Baker sounds tired. "Aftershocks can be worse than the earthquake. Get under your desk before something falls."

Emma studies the ceiling.

"Under your desk, Emma. *now*," Ms. Baker shouts as our desks begin to bounce again.

* * *

"Is it safe?" I ask as I approach Brendan in the parking lot.

Brendan slides off the hood of the car. "It's California. There's no such thing as safe."

"I mean, should we be driving?"

"They let us out of school, didn't they? They must've decided the coast is clear. I think the aftershocks have stopped. Besides, there's no bridges or tunnels between here and home. If Mother Nature decides to rock our world again, I'll pull over. Happy?"

"Ecstatic." I slide into the passenger side. "Have you heard from anyone at home?"

"Not yet." Brendan and I are quiet until he turns the car into our driveway.

I take my time getting my backpack. Brendan can go first and pave the way through whatever's waiting. He opens the door and steps in. Aunt Lily's shouting from my room.

"... for once... me... going back... Wyoming... I mean it."

Brendan whispers to me, "It's coming for you, Barbara."

"I thought Mom yelling at me about postpartum was the *thing*."

Brendan shakes his head. "It's a big steaming pile. One dinner of Mom blaming you isn't unusual. Mom on maternity leave with Aunt Lily and Grandma in the house... You get the stench of a very large load."

"What should we do?"

"Why do you always think you can fix things?" Brendan looks at me. "You can't fix these people. If Aunt Lily wants to leave, let's help her pack."

I put my backpack down. "It'd be nice to have my bedroom back."

"I'll check on Aunt Lily." Brendan opens his eyes wide. "You go see Grandma. She likes you."

"Well, somebody has to."

Brendan gives me a talk-to-the-hand salute and walks toward my bedroom. I head toward Brendan and Eric's room.

"Grandma, what're you doing?" I ask.

"I'm so happy you're safe." Grandma hugs me. "I was scared for you and Brendan."

"It wasn't a bad earthquake, 4.9 or 5.2. That's moderate to light. In science, we used our phones to collect information while under our desks. The teacher recorded what we found. Tomorrow we're going to put all the information into a presentation."

"See?" Grandma smiles. "Education's a blessing."

"So, what're you doing?"

Grandma frowns. "Packing. Lily and I are going home as soon as possible."

"Why? I mean... Aunt Lily was... I don't know what I'm saying."

"Lily doesn't feel safe." Grandma hangs her head. "I have to go with her."

"Why? Do you have to leave? Who'll help me make the Thanksgiving meal we talked about?"

"I'm sure your mother will bounce back and be ready

to cook."

"It's only a week away. I'm not so sure."

Grandma nods. "Positive thinking, Linn. Believe and good things will happen."

"Has positive thinking ever roasted a turkey?" I look around. "Where's Eric?"

"In your mom's room. I took him in there after the earthquake." Grandma smiles at me. "A mother's love is the strongest protection I can think of."

I almost laugh at the idea of Mom having love power. "I'm going to check on them."

A few minutes later I carry Eric into the foyer and grab my backpack.

"Might as well leave it there," Brendan complains. "Aunt Lily's not out of your room yet. She needs to polish her broom and call the flying monkeys. We should stay out of the way and hope she doesn't rip the stuffing out of us."

"That bad?" I ask.

"Yep. If I thought it would help, I'd toss a bucket of water on her." Brendan looks at Eric. "Speaking of flying monkeys... what's Baby Bubbles doing?"

"Grandma took him to Mom. When I checked, she was asleep and he was awake. I picked him up to check his diaper. He's clean but he won't let me put him down."

"He's two weeks old. How can he not let you put him down? Plop his diapered ass into the crib. You're so lame, even a baby succubus can manipulate you."

"If you read more mythology, you'd know..." I sigh. "A succubus is a female demon. They use sex to control men. Eric would be an incubus. Male."

Brendan stares at me. "First, I'm not convinced Bubbles there is male. Are you positive his *baby parts* won't change? I saw a show about it. Second, who says sex with a female demon is bad? Not me."

"Finished?" I ask.

"Yes," Brendan says. "And my timing's impeccable."

I'm confused until I hear the garage door open and Dad's voice ring out. "Bella? Brendan? Linn? Everyone all right?"

"Timing's everything." Brendan grins at me. "That's how you win an argument—make your point and move on before anyone can respond." He begins to walk out of the foyer.

"Winning requires facts," I say to Brendan's back.

"Last word, Spaz, last word."

I look at Eric resting in my arms. He focuses on me. "At least I have you," I coo.

An unmistakable sound comes from his backside followed by a foul smell.

"Seriously?"

* * *

"Thanks for nothing," I complain to my curtains. "Since Grandma and Aunt Lily left, you'd think I could get one decent night's sleep—just one! I need my brain to shut up!" Dragging myself out of bed, I bend over. "Pull it together. You can't skip school for a stomach ache." I reconsider and head for the bathroom.

Oh no.

Brendan shouts through my bathroom door. "Mom says to hurry up and eat breakfast."

"Tell Mom I need to talk to her," I call back.

"You okay?" Brendan asks.

"Get Mom," I shout.

Brendan grumbles as he leaves. Sitting on the floor I pull my knees up and try not to cry.

"What's going on?" Mom's voice drifts through the door.

"I'm bleeding," I whine. "From... there."

"I'll get some supplies," Mom responds matter-of-factly.

I wait and wonder why Mom doesn't know this is a big f-ing deal for me.

Finally, she knocks. "It's open."

Mom hands me two boxes. "I keep them under my sink in our bathroom."

"What do I do with these?" I ask.

"Read the labels and follow the directions." Mom moves back toward the bathroom door. "You still need some breakfast. Brendan will be leaving soon, so don't dawdle."

"Mom," I moan. "It hurts. Can I stay home?"

Mom's lip curls. "Suck it up. Women have done this since the beginning of time. It's the last day before Thanksgiving break, so you can handle one day in an air-conditioned building." She pulls the door shut.

I grab her supply boxes and stand slowly, speaking to the mirror. "You're on your own. Oh, wait. You have labels to help you. How thoughtful." I sit on the toilet to read.

When I stumble out of the back rooms, Brendan glances up from the table. "I've packed some toast for you." He holds up a sandwich bag with bread. "Let's get out of here before Mom returns."

I follow him out and fall into the car.

A few minutes later he looks sideways at me. "Have you got everything you need?"

"No!" I can't stop the angry words from pouring out. "I don't have a baseball bat."

"Why do you need a bat?" Brendan asks.

"So I can beat everyone senseless," I shout.

"Okay?" he responds carefully.

Brendan's kindness is infuriating. "You don't understand. No matter how much I try to be reasonable, it feels like I'm losing it. I hate this, I hate being a girl." I put my head down and cry. I cry because of the pain. I cry about my inability to hold it together and my fear of being like

Mom. I cry for the motherless child I know I am.

Brendan drives the rest of the way without talking. He parks the car and looks at me. "I can leave the keys if you need more time."

"I'm fine," I lie and wipe the tears away.

"I can carry your backpack."

"No!" I say in a panic. "I don't want anyone to know I'm having a period."

"L-Linn," Brendan stammers. "It's not your fault. You don't have to be perfect."

I scowl at Brendan. "Don't say it. I'm not Mom!"

"You're nothing like her. Let's get through today. Break starts tomorrow."

I open the car door. "See you after school." I stand and walk in what I hope's a straight line. I know Brendan's watching. *I'm not weak.*

Today I lack energy. I hobble into band and hide in the back row. I pull out my phone and pretend to take a call. I want to avoid Steve. After math, I duck into the bathroom and struggle with the supplies. As I walk into English, sweat's dripping from my forehead.

Ms. Hess walks to the front of the class. "Since we only have one day of school this week, I thought we'd play games."

People clap until Ms. Hess holds up her hand. "English games." She waits as the applause changes to groans. "Turn your chairs into clusters of four. Each group will create riddles or hinky-pinkies related to the books we've been reading. Remember, hinky-pinkies are two rhyming words with each word containing two syllables. Not to be confused with Pinkertons." Ms. Hess waits for a laugh. "Pinkertons? The detectives?" She glances around the room. "Never mind. At the end of class, I'll collect your puzzles and post the best ones online. You can earn extra credit by providing the correct answers."

I turn my desk. I love vocabulary games, but my brain isn't functioning. I groan when another cramp grips me and I put my head down.

* * *

"Linn?" Ms. Hess shakes me gently. "Linn, honey, are you there?"

"Fine," I mumble. I lift my head and wipe drool from my mouth. Ms. Hess and Ms. Garcia are standing by my desk. There're no students in the classroom. I try to jump up but I'm too uncoordinated. "What happened? Where? I don't know..."

Ms. Hess holds me back. "It's okay. I think you passed out. I called the office."

I see Ms. Garcia and panic sets in. "I'm fine. Really. I'm not sick. I've got to get going. My next class..." I look at the clock on the wall. "I'm late."

"You're not fine," Ms. Garcia says. "You passed out at school. This concerns us. I have an incident report for your parents. I'm guessing it's your period."

I remember this morning and realize why I feel sticky. "Oh crap." I consider the kind women in the room, knowing my face is red. The truth blurts out of me. "Today's my first period and everything I do hurts."

Ms. Hess pats my back. "Did you take anything for the pain?"

"No," I moan. "I didn't know it would hurt."

"Don't worry," Ms. Hess says. "Ask your doctor what to do. And remember, menstruation is not a weakness. It happens to the best of us. And the weaker sex—" she checks the room "—men... react poorly. So ignore them."

If I didn't like Ms. Hess so much, I'd laugh. I try to nod my head seriously.

"I called your mother and she said to have Brendan drive you home," Ms. Garcia says.

"Brendan? Home?" My panic's back at the thought of... everything.

"I've asked one of the girls in the office to get a sweater out of the lost and found. You can tie it around your waist," Ms. Garcia explains. "Once you get home, I'm going to call and check on you. Passing out is a medical concern."

"But..." I struggle to explain. "Mom... the baby... can't..."

Ms. Garcia stops me. "I've already explained the situation. Your mom understands."

Before I can think of a response, Sonja enters the room with a dark hoodie in her hand. "Ah," Ms. Garcia says. "Here's my girl. Thank you, Sonja."

Sonja walks over to me. "Here, Linn. Stand up and I'll help you with the hoodie."

"I'm sorry, Sonja. You shouldn't have to do this."

"Someone did the same for me once and I want to pay it forward. Besides, who better to help than me?" Sonja winks at me. "Come on, stand up."

I slide out of the desk carefully.

Sonja hands me the hoodie. "Wrap this around you and tie the sleeves in front. Then tuck the hoodie under you when you sit."

Ms. Garcia steps forward and looks at my new outfit. "Once you're home you can wash your clothes and the hoodie in cold water. I'm pretty sure that's been in lost and found for over a year. Nobody has claimed it, I'd say it's yours to keep."

"I need to clean the seat." I'm sure I've gone redder than ever before.

"Don't worry." Ms. Hess heads toward her desk. "I have gloves and disinfectant wipes."

The classroom door opens and Brendan walks in. Sonja and Ms. Garcia both step toward him. I look back at Ms. Hess. "I'm sorry. Don't you have another class?"

"No, this's my free period and then I have lunch. I

asked for two free classes in a row. That way I have time for my students. If you ever want to talk, I'm here." Ms. Hess's words cause me to tear up.

"Thanks." I walk toward Brendan and Sonja. "Sorry, can we go home now?"

"Sure, let's go." Brendan takes my backpack and walks toward the door.

I wait for the inevitable "Spaz," but it remains unspoken. Glancing at Sonja, I wonder if I should follow this new—nicer—Brendan. Sonja moves her hand, shooing me toward the door. Somehow, knowing Sonja trusts 'Nicer Brendan' is reassuring.

Brendan and I walk slowly to the car, and he opens the door for me. *Who is this guy?* I sit down being careful to keep the hoodie under me.

Brendan speaks without meeting my eyes. "Sonja and Ms. Garcia said passing out isn't a good sign. They think you need to see a doctor."

I lean my head on the car window. "Okay," I respond. I want to ask if Brendan and Sonja are dating but I don't have the energy.

"Linn?" Brendan gently shakes my shoulder. "We're home."

"Home?" I look around groggily.

"Don't worry, I'll get your backpack."

I walk in the front door and stop to listen. Eric must be napping. Maybe I can get to my room and change out of these clothes without...

"Garcia called." Mom's speech is slightly slurred. "A little blood and you fall apart."

"Stop it," Brendan demands. "She passed out. It's not something she can control."

"Passed out?" Mom sneers. "She wanted an excuse to skip school."

I open my mouth to respond but Brendan stops me.

"You can't win," he whispers. "Go clean up, I'll put this situation to bed."

"Thanks," I reply softly. "I'll grab a few more supplies and take a shower." I walk past Mom and check in Eric's room. *How does he sleep through arguments, yet stay awake all night?* I enter my parent's bathroom, lock the door behind me, and begin looking through the drawers on Mom's side. Finding a couple of new tubes of SPF lotion, I grab one. She'll never notice and I can always blame Brendan. I finally find a collection of pads and tampons under her sink. I lean down to reach the box in the back and freeze. The half-empty wine jug hidden behind the tampons explains a lot.

* * *

"Linn?" Dad knocks on my door. "Can I come in?"

Now what? "It's open."

Dad sits on the bed. "We missed you at dinner. Are you feeling better?"

"I took some ibuprofen, so it doesn't hurt anymore. I don't feel like eating but I haven't passed out again."

"Your mother says you're being dramatic and probably fell asleep at school."

"Dad! I passed out. How many times have you known me to be dramatic?"

Dad squirms. "What I know is, your mother needs support. She's having a tough time with the baby and maternity leave."

"And drinking too much," I add without thinking.

"Stop! Your mother doesn't have a drinking problem."

"Of course not," I say sarcastically. "If we don't name it, the problem doesn't exist."

Dad stands and holds his hands in fists by his side. "I'm going to pretend you didn't say that. Once you're sensible, you might remember your mother and I provide everything. The house, food, your clothes—it's all because of us. When she was your age, your mother worked the potato fields. You are too privileged to appreciate that fact."

"Dad, having a period doesn't make me less sensible. I know—"

"Not another word," Dad interrupts. "Do you hear me?" He turns and storms out.

I grab my journal as the tears begin to fall.

* * *

Journal Entry – Thankful for Found Mothers

Being a girl sucks. My first period hurt. They're called cramps. Your abdomen seizes up and every part of you wants to go into the fetal position. I continue to hope for a good mother. I was thinking I would get some help from her, but no! She's never going to help me! Useless! What are mothers for if they won't help you be a girl? Mom's hidden jug explains a lot. It's better if I'm not worthy because Mom's drunk, not because I'm unlovable. I thought I was an un-mothered child, but I've got mothers at school. Ms. Hess and Ms. Garcia. Even Sonja's more caring than my mother.

Grandma Rose was wrong. Mom didn't pull it together and make Thanksgiving dinner. Dad went to the grocery store and bought pre-cooked food. Not a great meal, but not the worst served in this house. I was thankful to survive the day without being blamed for everything, and my period stopped. Not looking forward to the next one!

L.E.A.P

<u>LEAP</u>
I'm reconsidering my LEAP list. I think it needs more definitions or items.

LEAP List Reconsidered

Growth spurt - ✔

Body development - ✔✔

Start period - ✔✔✔

I'm thinking 3 isn't really done. Periods aren't going to stop. Developmental stuff continues until you get old, so pretty much forever. The Valley Girl articles made it sound like you only have to grow and reach your adult body development. Now I've started having periods and I know there are more things to worry about.

Medical Issues – Sonja says I need to see a doctor and find out what's wrong with me. Well, she didn't say it that way. I know I need to find out what's wrong. Ha, that's a question I've been asking my entire life.

Sex – What happens? When does it happen? If there's something wrong with me during my period, can I have sex?

Pregnancy – In case I do have sex (ever), I do not want to get pregnant. I already have to take care of Eric and my mother. I don't need another baby.

Maybe all these combine into one issue—being a girl. I hate what happens to girls as they grow up but I don't want to be a boy.

BE SELF-SUFFICIENT
This isn't all about getting a license or having money or getting out of the house. I'm already self-sufficient. I realize I've been working on this since I was young. Each time Mom got drunk, I became more self-sufficient. The marbles taught me to be self-sufficient. I was determined to be my own person and not allow anyone to control me.

DATING AND PREFERENCE
I need to know who, what, when, where, and why. The answer to why had better be an amazingly good reason.

FIND YOUR IDENTITY
I don't need to become my own person—I already am who I am.

My identity does include being a liar. I'm not sorry about this. I'm not supposed to say Mom drinks too much. I'm not supposed to say Mom has postpartum depression. I'm supposed to act like I'm perfect and our entire house is perfect. Well, it's not. I'm a liar and I was taught to be one!

HAVE THREE GOOD FRIENDS, BELONG
I only have two good friends. Joining the Key Club helped me meet people but not make friends. Who decided three is the magic number,

anyway? I'm happy to have Nadine and Alan. I don't feel like I'm missing out on something by not having another good friend. I don't know if I can count Brendan, Sonja, or Steve as friends yet.

FEEL SAFE
This is a huge issue! The only time I felt safe in this house was when Grandma Rose and I were alone. She made me <u>love toast</u> and we talked.

Isn't love part of feeling safe? Or is being safe part of love? The Valley Girl articles didn't say anything about love. But Grandma makes toast and I feel both safe and loved. Dad says he loves all of his family members equally. He also says we should all do our part to take care of the people we love. But he doesn't follow his own advice. He takes care of Mom, so I think he loves her. If Dad really loved Brendan and me, wouldn't he do something to take care of us too? Wouldn't he get Mom some help so we could feel safe?

I started this list about six months ago and all I can say is... what was I thinking? Growing up takes a lot more time and effort than I thought.

Linn

Walker

Gurke

Chapter 14
Home for the Holidays

PACKING MY CLARINET AFTER the Winter Concert, I head for the front of the school. I'm not in a hurry to start my holiday break since it means being home. Mom has been at home since Eric was born last month. Her maternity leave will last until April, but she's not well. Dad stays with her whenever possible. I think he's making sure Mom isn't alone with Eric. That way she can't harm the baby. Still, no one is allowed to say anything about her issues. Eric and postpartum aren't the only reason my parents didn't show for my concert. They've created excuses to avoid my events since Brendan learned to drive. But that doesn't work today. Brendan's not home so he can't drive me. Still, Fault-line Linn isn't worth their time.

Standing by the front of Firestorm, I watch Mom drive past the entrance. Mom knows how to drive to one place. I figure she'll arrive at work in the next five minutes and realize she's in the wrong place. Will she remember to pick me up on her way home?

"I have got to get my driver's license as soon as possible," I say to the night sky.

Should I walk onto the road and flag her down? Before I start, Steve walks up behind me.

He whispers in my ear, "Hey, Gurke. What ya doing?"

I roll my eyes. "Waiting for my ride."

"Wanna give me a kiss?"

I turn to look at Steve but it's dark. "Why would I do

that?" I ask.

"'Cause my lips are still puffed up."

I'm NOT going closer. "What are you talking about?"

Steve smiles and I can see the white of his teeth. "Tuba player—a few minutes of blowing my brass baby and my lips are soft and kissable." Steve's voice turns serious. "Emma and I are friends. We aren't dating. I would do anything for her, but not kissing. I'd rather—"

I cut Steve off before he says something I don't want to hear. "Emma's a good person. She would be a fantastic girlfriend." I stand up straighter, proud I defended her.

Steve follows as I walk forward. "Didn't your parents come to the concert?"

"No," I say. "They have a baby to take care of. What about your parents?"

"They went to my brother Billy's play at the elementary school. Isn't Brendan here?"

I reach the sidewalk and realize I'm trapped in an even smaller area with Steve. "Brendan and Javy went to check out a college. They won't be home until tomorrow."

"Who's coming to get you?"

"Does it matter?" I bark. "Leave me alone."

"I saw your mom drive past a few minutes ago and thought you might need a ride."

I feel bad for losing my cool with Steve when he was being helpful. I turn toward him and begin to apologize but my mouth isn't working.

Mom pulls to a stop at the curb and beeps the horn. I turn to the road and open the passenger door. "Hurry up," she says, "your father needs help with Eric."

"Can we give Steve a ride?" I ask. "He lives close to us."

Mom leans down and looks at Steve. Her face moves into a sneer. "I told you to stay away from his type. Now get in."

I turn to Steve. "Sorry, we can't—"

"Linn, let's go!" Mom's shout interrupts what I'm sure would be a sincere apology.

I plop into the front and barely get my door closed before Mom pulls the car forward in a jerking motion. I brace myself on the dash. I grab the seat belt and click it home. Glancing back, I see Mrs. Miller pull up to Steve.

"Sorry," I mumble.

Mom thinks I'm talking to her. "You should be sorry," she agrees. "I do everything for you without so much as a thank you. And your brother..."

I turn my brain to low and respond with murmurs. Whatever Mom's saying doesn't matter. As soon as we walk in the house and see Dad, it'll be sweetness and light. I'll pretend this tirade never happened. *Mom's perfect, I'm perfectly happy... blah, blah, blah.*

* * *

In my dream, a tiger stalks toward me with her head lowered. She crouches and studies me—deciding which bite will be the juiciest. I can't move. "Wake up, Spaz," she growls. Confusion flows through my subconscious. I'm going to be dinner, but she's not threatening? The tiger launches herself toward me. My body shakes as her claws sink into me. I sit up screaming.

"Chillax Bubbles. It's just us."

I open my eyes to find Brendan standing over my bed. His hand is exactly where the tiger grabbed my shoulder. "What're you doing?" I attempt to clear the dream and my fear.

"We're back from our trip and brought you a Christmas tree. Want to help us decorate?"

I groan and fall back onto my pillow.

Brendan continues, "Mom and Dad took the baby and went to the Kaplans' house. I thought you'd be happy we let you sleep in. Why were you screaming?"

"It was a dream... nightmare. There was a tiger..." *Suddenly my brain understands the words Brendan has been using... us... our... we... I'm wide awake now.* I look around my room and swallow. "Javy?"

"Hey, Linn." Javy gives me a small wave from behind Brendan. "Hope we didn't scare you." *He should run screaming out of the house—it's what I want to do.*

I lower my voice to a whisper and put as much warning into it as I can. "Brendan... let me get dressed. I'll meet you in the living room."

Brendan turns red. *Even after everything that happened last month, is this the first time he's realized I'm a girl? I'm pretty sure Javy knows.*

I pull the covers over my head and wait until the door shuts. I peek out of my bed tent to make sure I'm alone. "Disaster," I announce to myself. "More than a fault line... a complete disaster." I open my closet and glance in the mirror. I imagine it smirking at me. "I know, I know," I sigh. "This guy'll never date a disaster like me. I don't care." I pull the sweater over my head and correct my statement. "Okay, that was a lie, I do care."

After locking the bathroom door, I pee, wash my hands, and splash my face with water. I run a brush through my tangled mess of hair. I head toward the smell of fresh-cut evergreen.

A roll of glowing tree lights sits on top of our indoor decoration storage crate.

Brendan's lying on the ground, adjusting the screws in the stand.

Javy's giving directions from across the room. "Tighten the left a little more. No, your other left... That's getting there."

"What's for breakfast?" I ask.

Brendan answers from under the tree. "You slept through breakfast, wait for lunch."

I open the pantry and grab an oatmeal bar. After one bite I open the fridge and reach for the milk. "How does anyone eat this? It tastes like cardboard." I pour the milk into a glass and walk back into the living room while reading the wrapper. "Do these things taste bad because they're gluten-free?" I'm rambling again.

Javy looks at the wrapper I'm carrying and answers, "Oatmeal is naturally gluten-free. The company brags because gluten-free is the new hotness. Consumers think they're getting special treatment. But they're paying more for the feeling of being healthy. Those bars are no better than having oatmeal with blueberries. Unless the factory uses the same machinery to process wheat and doesn't clean it."

I stare at Javy with my mouth open. "How do you know that?" I mumble.

"I read a lot. I'm considering college chemistry programs. I want to specialize in foodborne illnesses." He turns back to the tree. "Linn, is it straight?"

Normally I would mess with Brendan while he's stuck on the ground, but I'm thinking about Javy's gluten comment. *Have I been viewing Javy as a stereotype? Assuming the Golden Boy can't be smart? If a boy has abs, does that make him shallow?*

Brendan's voice cuts into my thoughts. "Linn! Is the tree straight?"

I decide to be nice. "Looks straight to me. We'll need to cut the top branch a little. But otherwise, it's great."

Brendan slides away from the base and stands up. A small sprig of pine needles is stuck in his not-so-perfect hair. I walk toward the roll of lights without saying anything. I unplug the lights and carry them to the tree. Brendan and I automatically stand on either side of the tree and begin to pass the string of bulbs.

Javy watches us for a minute. "What can I do?"

Brendan nods his head at the ornament crate. "We left a timer and extension cord in there. Plug it in and set it to turn on around five and off at midnight."

Javy switches on the timer and we stand back to admire our work.

"Pretty good, don't ya think?" Brendan asks. "Now for the ornaments."

"Aren't you going to wait for your parents?" Javy asks.

Brendan glances at me with a shut-the-fuck-up face. He turns to his friend. "They used to help, but over the years, it's become a sibling tradition. We'd wait for Eric, but he can't walk yet so..."

I pull ornament boxes out of the crate and place them on the coffee table. "Remember," I say to Brendan, "take the first ornament you touch and describe where it came from." I consider Javy standing to one side. "If you want to help, you can pick an ornament and decide which of us has to tell its story."

Javy laughs. "I'll watch from a safe distance before I jump into this bizarr-o rivalry."

"Okay then..." I place my hand on an ornament box and look at Brendan. "You ready?"

Brendan covers his eyes dramatically. "Go for it."

I open the lid and we each grab an ornament and head toward the tree. I stop and check the soft gingerbread person in my hand. "Grandma Rose made these and gave ten to our family about five years ago. We have three left." I hang the ornament on the tree.

Brendan holds a decoration up and smiles. "It's a baseball player. Mom and Dad gave it to me when I made the high school team."

For the next thirty minutes we hang ornaments and recount where they come from.

Eventually, Javy picks up two ornaments that have our birth years painted on them and moves forward. "These are from when you were born. Added by... your mother?" Javy looks between us to see if his guess's right.

"No," Brendan answers, "those are from the Kaplans. They're Jewish but they celebrate Christmas, sort of."

Javy gestures to Brendan. "Hey, what about the ornament we bought for Linn yesterday? It's still in the car. I'll go get it."

Javy heads out the front door.

I turn to Brendan, "Awww, you bought me a gift? How sweet."

Brendan peers at me from under his eyelashes. "I have to tell you." He sighs. "Before I left for the campus visit, Dad told me how much college's going to cost. California schools are reasonable. But our family's in a difficult situation. Dad says we have to cut costs."

"What does that have to do with Christmas ornaments?" I ask.

"Dad gave me money to buy this tree but told me we won't have money for gifts this year. The ornament's all you're getting from me." Brendan pauses. "Possibly all you'll get from anyone in this house. And if you want to give a gift, it'll have to be homemade."

"What about Eric? Will they buy him presents?"

"Dad said Eric's too young to notice. He laughed when he said Eric's age gives them a free year. They don't have to buy him anything. So..." Brendan sweeps his hand to indicate the tree, "Merry Christmas. You got a tree."

I smile at Brendan's humor. "And you've become a tree." I point to the pine needles clinging to his hair. I'm still laughing at Brendan's rush to the mirror when Javy walks back in.

"Linn," Javy says, "a guy is sitting out front. He needs to see you."

"A guy? And he wants to see me?"

Javy lowers his voice. "I tried to talk to him. He just

said your name."

I head to the front. Checking the side window, I can see a boy sitting on the steps. His face in his hands and his back shaking. *I recognize crying when I see it.* Slipping on my tennis shoes, I open the door, walk out, and sit next to the hunched figure.

"Steve? What's wrong?"

His voice quivers when he responds. "I'm a worthless piece of shit."

"That's *not* true," I say. "Everybody I know thinks you're a great guy."

Steve's head snaps up and he looks at me with red-rimmed eyes. "Well, you don't know my father, now do you?" He throws the words at me.

"No... I've never met him, but I'm sure..."

Steve interrupts me with a harsh laugh that turns into a shout. "In all the sappy Christmas movies everyone has a perfect family, but not me. I don't deserve a loving household 'cause nobody can love me."

"Steve, you're—"

"Don't say it. Don't be like everyone else. Don't fucking lie to me, Linn." Steve drops his head back into his hands and makes a growling noise.

"Okay, no lies," I whisper. "You tell me what's happening and I'll listen. I promise." When he doesn't speak, I reach out and touch his shoulder. Steve flinches in pain. My mind races in too many directions. *Is he hurt? Who did this? Is this abuse? Is this why Billy hides behind Steve?* "Steve... did someone hurt you?"

"How do you do it?" Steve asks and glances at me.

"How do I do what?"

Steve's face reminds me of the bull that used to be on Grandma Rose's farm right before it charged. "You know... how do you live with a drunk?"

My mouth drops open in surprise. "I... don't..." I shake

my head.

"Remember, no lies," Steve demands.

"I... I didn't think you knew," I moan.

"Linn, everyone knows. You're the only person who thinks it's a secret."

I feel defensive. "Well, you're better at keeping a secret than I am... which parent?"

"My father."

"Is he a mean drunk?"

"What the hell do you think?" Steve snarls. "He's as mean as your mother and he's stronger."

"My mother doesn't hurt me."

"Oh, please." Steve rolls his eyes at me. "Not all hurt comes with bruises."

"But your shoulder—"

"I'm not talking about my shoulder," he shouts. "End of discussion."

"Okay, you're right." *I've never seen this Steve. How far will anger take him? I decide it's best to speak carefully.* "Have you looked for help?"

Steve jumps up and stands over me. "Have you?"

"No," I admit. "I guess I'm scared... I'm... chicken."

"That's two of us." Steve peeks at the windows on either side of the door. "Brendan's watching us. And... what's his name? The soccer dude."

"Javy," I answer and turn to the door. Both pull back when they see me looking.

"I thought I only had to worry about your mom calling the cops." Steve relaxes. "What about those two? Are they going to kick my ass? Soccer style?"

"Ignore them. Please, sit back down, and let's work this out."

Steve sighs and sits next to me. "I... just wanted to talk to somebody. But I'm not going to say anything to get my dad in trouble. I can't report him and have our family lose its only income. I have to think about Mom and Billy. They need Dad... and me."

"I don't know. I've got more questions than answers. I can't do anything—"

"I didn't ask you to DO anything."

"Okay. You didn't. I get it."

"Answer this... do you worry?"

I laugh, but it's not funny. "Where should I start?"

"Do you think you will be a drunk, like your mother?"

I think about Steve's question. "I used to worry. I mean, I share her DNA, and if it's genetic... But I've stopped worrying. I'm *not* Mom and I'll never become her."

"How do you know you're not like her?"

"Recently I realized Mom doesn't care about anyone except herself, Dad, and the bottle. I care about people more than alcohol. I want to help people. Like Brendan, Nadine, Alan, Eric..." I look directly at Steve. "And you. I know you don't feel safe at home, but you have friends and you're safe with us. Plus, the word *safety* means being loved."

"Really, Linn?"

"Yes. We're friends. You're safe and loved with me." I laugh softly. "Not kissing type love, but secure and cared for."

"Well, that's both disappointing and good at the same time." Steve glances sideways. "So, how do I know if I'm like Dad or not?"

"You have to take the Linn test. Ready?"

"I hope so. What's that?"

"Simple. Name something you can't live without. Not a person, but a thing you might be addicted to... Gambling? Drinking? Drugs?"

"Donuts," Steve says immediately.

"Donuts?" I ask. "You think you're addicted to donuts?"

"Oh, yes. I love, love, love donuts. I think about donuts

all the time. Once, Emma bought me a dozen donuts. I didn't share with her, Billy, or anyone. I'm a donut fiend!"

"Okay... we'll go with donuts. Here's the situation. I'm going to buy you donuts. Not just one dozen, but boxes and boxes of donuts. Then I'll put them at the end of this driveway. Do you want them?"

"Yes!"

"You want all of them? Even the ones with coconut?"

"Absolutely."

"Now, I'm going to put your brother Billy between you and the donuts."

"Billy? I told you. I don't want to share with Billy... at least not donuts."

"Oh, you don't have to share." I consider Steve for a moment. "But if you want those donuts, you have to hurt Billy."

Steve waves his hands in front of me. "No. I won't hurt Billy."

"Are you sure?" I ask. "Remember, you can have all the donuts. But if you don't hurt Billy, you get nothing."

"No, I'm sure. I wouldn't ever hurt Billy. Geez, Linn, who would do that?"

"An addict would, Steve." I shake my head. "What would your father do if it was alcohol and not donuts? I know my mother would tear through me to get to those bottles."

Steve wipes his eyes. "I'm sorry, Linn."

"Don't be sorry. It's not your fault."

"Back to square one. What can we do?"

"I don't know. I'm beginning to believe I can't fix my mother. I can only work on myself. And I know someone who might help. There's a teacher at school who'll listen."

"No teachers." Steve's voice goes up an octave. "They have to report things. You agreed, no reporting anyone so I don't get kicked out of the house."

"Don't worry, I know all the teacher's rules. She won't need to report us."

"Which teacher?"

"Ms. Hess, my English teacher. I'm pretty sure she'll keep it quiet."

"What if she isn't as cool as you think?"

We sit quietly for a few minutes searching our brains.

"What if we talk around the problem," I suggest. "You know, we don't say anything exactly but hint at it. If Ms. Hess's cool, we'll know by her response."

Steve checks his watch. "I guess we can try, after Winter Break."

"That'll give us time to work on what to say." I consider my next words. "Will you... I mean... break is more than two weeks... Oh crap—will you be safe?"

Steve shakes his head. "I'll try not to piss my dad off."

"Steve, you're not responsible for this."

"Still, I need to check on Billy." Steve glances at the door. "And soccer dude's waiting."

I think for a minute. "He's not important right now."

Steve smiles. "Are you thinking I'm more important?"

"You matter. I told you that, but I need to take care of Eric. Just like you have Billy, I need to help Eric. Come back over the break."

"So your mom can call the cops? Thanks, but no thanks. I'll text you." Steve gives me a small wave and walks away.

I watch his retreating back and think about everything said and things avoided. *I know Mom and Dad won't stay away forever.* Glancing at my watch, I stand up and turn back to the house. Brendan and Javy are still at the front door windows.

"Are you okay?" Brendan asks as I walk inside.

I keep walking toward the living room. "I'm fine. Honestly, this time, I'm fine."

They both follow me. "What did Steve want?"

"He just needed to talk." I look at our Christmas tree. "We did a great job. Thanks for bringing it home, guys."

Javy steps up next to me. "Linn, if you need anything... I'd be glad to help."

"I'm fine." I smile at Javy. "I can't fix everything, but I can take care of myself... and Eric." I turn and walk out of the room. I need to find my journal.

I do care about Steve, and I want to help him, even when he's annoying. I'm pretty sure I can be that person. And I can list Steve as one of my good friends. Without dating him.

* * *

Journal Entry – Eric's First Christmas

Dear Eric,

I know you can't read yet—but this journal entry is for you. I want to tell you everything I have learned—mostly in the last few months. When you are older, I give you permission to read my entire journal. Just you! Don't share this with anyone else in our family—even Brendan.

At some point in your life, Dad will tell you the difference between a want and a need. He will say you only <u>need</u> air, water, a home, food, and clothes. Our parents will make sure you have the basic needs. But there are needs Dad doesn't include in his list.

LINN'S EMERGING ADULT PLAN

Like it or not—you need to grow up. You won't get any help from Mom and only a little from Dad. I hope Dad's better at helping a boy grow up than he was with a girl. Either way, you can't avoid getting older.

You need to be self-sufficient. This isn't just learning to drive. Driving's important—so you can get out of the house. Becoming self-sufficient requires a lot more, like learning to cook—don't eat anything Aunt Lily serves! I'm still working on being self-sufficient and I'll let you know when I figure out the rest.

You need to have friends—good friends. Friends who will support you, listen to your fears, and help you belong. It's easy to tell yourself nobody understands and you will never have friends. But that's not true. You may find a friend in someone you don't like in the beginning. Be willing to let people grow on you.

You need to feel safe. I know this is next to impossible with our parents. Dad can't be trusted and Mom isn't equipped to be a parent. Unfortunately, we can't change who we were born to. Decide to trust. Just not everyone. Decide who will be your safe people.

Also, you should lie. I know it doesn't seem like the right thing to do, but I'm giving you permission to lie when you have to. For instance, at school, you shouldn't lie about where you got the answers for a test. But at home, lying's an important skill.

Basically—you need to survive this family.

MY PROMISE

I don't know about being a boy—but Brendan's advice probably isn't all that great. Relax, the physical stuff will happen in its own time. I'll try to help with the rest of the list.

I'll try to help you become self-sufficient.

I'll work at being your friend—despite being angry sometimes.

I'll be honest with you, even when I lie to others.

I'll support you and listen to what you want—and need.

I'll celebrate every birthday—no matter what type of trouble you get into.

I'll put ice on your visible injuries and help you understand the invisible scars.

I'll always think you are beautiful.

You're safe and loved with me.

I'm not perfect—and I'll make mistakes. No

matter what you hear in our house—there's no such thing as perfect. Still, you're a good person and deserve to be loved.

I will always love you.

Your sister,

Linn Walker Gurke

Author's Note

I wrote this book to acknowledge my biggest regret—allowing others to stop me from seeking help for my much younger brother and myself in dealing with our mother's alcoholism. Since beginning to write, I've learned a lot but I'm not an expert. So, consider that grain of salt before listening to me.

A few things I've learned:

Alcoholism is a whole family issue. It impacts everyone who lives in the house as well as your friends. It is not your fault, but it will change your behavior. Secrets and lies run rampant among these families. That's not the best way to deal with any problems. Seek help, look for information, and know you are not alone!

Alcoholism can also include one type of Mother Wound. In our society, mothers are held up as perfect people who love their children unconditionally and never do anything wrong. There is no such thing as perfect. Additionally, there are mothers who don't have the capacity to love or care for their children. People who grow up with an emotionally unavailable mother suffer from a Mother Wound.

Professional help is best for dealing with Alcoholism and/or a Mother Wound. However, I have also found writing to be cathartic—particularly when I am able to find humor in life. I can't change the past. But I can stop the cycle and share my thoughts with others.

Begin to seek help with this list and then expand and share beyond what I've learned.

L.E.A.P

https://www.mayoclinic.org/
https://www.psychologytoday.com/
https://www.motherwoundproject.com/
https://www.niaaa.nih.gov/alcohols-effects-health/
alcohols-effects-body
https://www.aa.org/   and   https://al-anon.org/
https://nacoa.org/
https://www.samhsa.gov/

About the Author

Toni Bellon moved to Georgia in 1991 with her husband. Presently, she lives in Johns Creek. As a child, Toni lived in California until her parents decided to move to Knoxville, Tennessee halfway through her high school years. Those years taught Toni that snarky humor was her best defense in the face of both confusion and anger.

As a way to help others deal with the uneven power dynamics between children and adults, Toni became a teacher. She left academia in 2014 to care for a mother who suffered from Dementia and Parkinson's. During that time, Toni started writing by using humor to present the darker side of shared human ordeals. She hopes to bring a smile to the audience and help lighten their load.

When she isn't writing, critiquing, or volunteering with the Atlanta Writers Club or A Novel Idea, Toni spends time in her new favorite role... Grandma.

Find out more at https://tonibellon.com/